THE CHELBECK CHARGER

The spring of 1816 finds wealthy Sir Ralph Marwood once again reluctantly fixed in town to find husbands for his daughters Emily and Sophia. When a chance encounter throws the dashing Piers Aubery in their path, he and his younger daughter Sophia are delighted. But Emily, who appears to be the prime object of Piers's attentions, cannot like him. She remains suspicious of Piers and his intentions, and her efforts to prevent a match are further complicated by the advent of the Chelbeck Charger.

Books by Audrey Blanshard
in the Linford Romance Library:

A SINGULAR ELOPEMENT
THE FEARNS OF AUDLEY STREET

AUDREY BLANSHARD

THE CHELBECK CHARGER

Complete and Unabridged

LINFORD
Leicester

First published in Great Britain in 1977 by
Robert Hale Limited
London

First Linford Edition
published 2001
by arrangement with
Robert Hale Limited
London

British Library CIP Data

Blanshard, Audrey
    The Chelbeck Charger.—Large print ed.—
Linford romance library
1. Love stories
2. Large type books
I. Title
823.9′14 [F]

ISBN 0–7089–4566–X

Published by
F. A. Thorpe (Publishing)
Anstey, Leicestershire

Set by Words & Graphics Ltd.
Anstey, Leicestershire
Printed and bound in Great Britain by
T. J. International Ltd., Padstow, Cornwall

This book is printed on acid-free paper

1

There was the customary press of people in the Exhibition Room at Somerset House in April of 1816 to view the Royal Academy canvases. For the expenditure of a shilling anyone, whether merchant, lawyer, clergy or squire up from the country with his lady, could fancy himself art critic. The Hon. Piers Aubrey, however, considered himself something of a cognoscente and the daubs, which graced the high walls in jumbled array, he thought decidedly inferior to the choice works of art which adorned his own, or — to be absolutely precise — his brother's house.

Still, there were amusing trifles to be met with here and he espied just such a one at that moment; raising his glass and stepping back the better to view the delicious curves of a trio of naked ladies, preserving their modesty with a single sinuous length of filmy gauze, he collided with a fellow admirer of the arts.

'A thousand pardons . . . ma'am!' he said, turning and finding himself contemplating two ladies at close quarters this time, fully-clad but no less delectable than the inanimate trio.

The young lady whom he had jostled was consulting her catalogue, but now raised her head and fixed him with brilliant blue eyes. A faint blush stained her cheek as the smiling gaze of the elegant stranger lingered a trifle too long. 'My fault entirely, sir, I was quite out of the world endeavouring to identify one of the landscapes.'

Piers' glance drifted briefly from the speaker to her companion, who was equally attractive but younger, plumper and, he hazarded, a trifle empty-headed: not that he had any particular partiality for Blue-stockings, but in present circumstances he supposed a conversation of an erudite nature would further his interests with the damsels more conformably than a frivolous approach. He returned his attention to the blue-eyed lady.

'Permit me to introduce myself,' he said, sweeping off his tall beaver hat to reveal cropped auburn curls which dwindled into sidewhiskers and finally disappeared beneath the ear-high snowy neckcloth. 'Piers Aubery at your service, ma'am. Perhaps I might assist you in your difficulty? I flatter myself I have a nodding acquaintance with the work of most of the better-known artists.'

This obliging speech drew a response from an unexpected quarter. 'Pleased to meet you, sir,' came the gruff tones of a hitherto unnoticed elderly gentleman, who had been leaning on his stick perusing the brushwork of some drapery with close attention. 'Ralph Marwood.' He held out his hand and favoured the young stranger with a look both searching and cautious. 'My daughters, Sophia and Emily, Mr Aubery,' he said after a pause, during which he appeared to assess with narrowed beetle-browed eyes the young man's worthiness of his daughter's acquaintance.

Piers, who had thought them unescorted, was a trifle disappointed but undeterred.

'Delighted,' he murmured, bowing low and noting that Miss Sophia was the younger sister and already fluttering her lashes at him. He pursued his conversation with Emily. 'Which landscape is puzzling you, ma'am, if you please?'

Miss Marwood indicated a canvas of modest proportions and placed bodkin between two impressive portraits — one of a bishop, the other a notable race-horse.

'Ah yes,' said Piers with evident assurance, taking up his glass again, 'that is certainly by Mr Constable — a little-known exponent of the brush, but . . . ' Here he hesitated a little before expressing an opinion, then seeing Miss Marwood's obvious appreciation of the work, he concluded,

4

' . . . it is delightful, is it not? — such freeness of composition, such colour.' He did not care one jot for its modern look, but what matter as long as he pleased the lady? 'I do agree, sir, he has indeed a most refreshing style,' Emily answered, smiling approval on both picture and critic.

'Fiddle-faddle!' cut in her father, Sir Ralph. 'What's amiss with the style of Claude and his school, tell me that! There's no . . . no order or shape to that thing!' he declared waving his stick at the offending picture and almost decapitating a short-sighted lady admirer of the bishop's likeness.

'Oh, nothing wrong with it at all, sir!' Piers hastened to agree, cursing himself for forgetting the tastes of the all-important parent. 'I have a keen appreciation of Claude myself,' (which was true) 'and *his* canvases are the ones to be purchased and admired for a life-time — but Mr Constable's scenes take the eye for a fleeting moment of pleasure.' He allowed himself the hint of a complicit smile to Miss Marwood. 'I think I may say in all modesty I am gathering together a pleasant little gallery of my own . . . choosing,' he concluded, the innocent gaze of Miss Marwood upon him suddenly compelling an unwonted veracity.

All at once a party of matrons swarmed about them with cries of 'My dear, what an exquisite frame — how I should like that for the parlour!' and 'Such a miserable likeness — why, my little Honoria could do better, I vow!'

'Shall we rest our weary limbs, my dears?' suggested Sir Ralph to his daughters: his lean bony frame looked as though it was plagued with the rheumatism. 'There is a temptingly vacant bench behind us. Join us if you will, sir, I should like to hear more of your collection.'

The quartet settled themselves in the centre of the thronged Exhibition Room, Piers flanked by Sir Ralph on one side, and Sophia and Emily on the other. Sophia had contributed nothing to the conversation but she clearly found the Hon. Piers Aubery vastly more interesting than any painting: she scarcely took her long-lashed gaze from his elegant attire and lively, handsome features. Indeed, Emily considered her sister's scrutiny to be bordering on the ill-bred and was about to divert her attention when her own was caught by the gentlemen's conversation.

' . . . Well, you must come to dine with us, then you may see the Claude, and judge for yourself its fineness. I'd be honoured if you'd bring your lady — and your daughters, of course.' Here he favoured both girls with a smile of devastating charm: few members of the opposite sex had ever been known to resist it. He extracted his card from a bejewelled case and handed it to Sir Ralph.

'Lady Marwood was taken from us these four years past,' the old gentleman explained, viewing the ostentatious case with a slightly jaundiced eye, 'but I'm sure my daughters and I would be most pleased to accept your very kind invitation. You are fixed . . . where?' he asked, peering at the card. 'Haven't got my reading spectacles.'

'Bittadon House, Grosvenor Street.'

'Ah!' cried Sir Ralph, looking under bushy brows at his young companion. 'So you will be Lord Bittadon's — '

' — Brother,' supplied Piers, not without a certain reluctance: he was doomed to play second fiddle to his elder brother, Roland, and it rankled — constantly. 'When shall we say, then?' he went on quickly to avoid any discussion of Roland's virtues — for that rankled even more. He made an elaborate performance of consulting a tablet which he drew from a back pocket, and which bore only the odds and stakes for the cock-fight he had attended the night before. Keeping it tilted away from the sharp-eyed Sophia and towards her myopic father, he ran a pencil down the jumbled figures. 'How would Friday suit, sir?'

Sir Ralph looked across Mr Aubery

and Sophia to his eldest daughter. 'Are we promised to anyone on Friday, my dear?'

'Not to my knowledge, papa,' Emily replied. Assuming her absentminded parent had not omitted to tell her of an engagement it was reasonable to suppose they were free: their social life was not of a hectic nature, in spite of its being the peak of the season.

'Friday, then?' said Piers making an impressive entry amidst the sporting arithmetic.

It was all arranged to everyone's satisfaction and as they made their way to the exit Piers asked if he might summon a hackney for the Marwoods.

'That is most kind, sir, but my landau should be waiting.'

Piers was pleased to hear that as it bespoke a man of comfortable circumstances: he was even more satisfied when he beheld the vehicle itself, which was stately, crested and, although old-fashioned, of undeniable magnificence; for that together with the coachman and two grooms suggested Sir Ralph Marwood was a warm man indeed.

Piers made his farewells to the party as the coachman, of an age with his master, urged the fine pair of chestnuts forward. Watching the landau disappear at a sedate pace along the overcast Strand he felt very content with the morning's work, and turning briskly on his heel walked with a jaunty step to his club.

★ ★ ★

His brother, Roland Aubery, the Right Hon. the Viscount Bittadon, had not enjoyed a rewarding morning: indeed, he expressed himself somewhat forcefully on that very subject to his twin sister, Harriet, when the morning-room door had scarcely closed upon their departing visitors.

'Where in Hades *is* that scapegrace gull-catcher brother of ours, do you suppose?'

Roland, at eight-and-twenty, was a tall, well-made man and his powerful frame was complemented by a fine head and not unhandsome features: the jaw was perhaps a little heavy — a trait he would not disguise with sidewhiskers as long as Piers sported them — and his hair was an unremarkable brown, but the whole face was transmuted by the attractive grey eyes which bespoke a disposition of both humour and gentleness.

They were neither gentle nor humorous, however, when Harriet glanced at him at that moment, and she knew from experience Piers was the one person able to make Roly look intimidating: she sighed and assumed her customary role as peace-maker between her brothers. 'I know his behaviour is beyond anything at times . . . ' She ignored the fraternal snort which greeted this remark. ' . . . But gullcatcher is a trifle harsh, is it not? He has scarcely *swindled* those two ladies.' She nodded towards the door to indicate the visitors who had just taken their leave. Her hair and eye colouring were identical with Roland's, but although she was a tall girl she had been spared the large-boned look of her twin. The younger pair of twin girls in the family, now married, were almost indistinguishable in looks and it was a source of relief to everyone that Harriet and Roland had not been equally indistinguishable twin boys: such dual confusion in one family would have been intolerable.

'No!' cried Roland, striding across to the window to watch for the return of the missing Piers, 'but you cannot deny he swindles *me* constantly!'

'Certainly he is naughty where money is con — '

'Naughty!' interrupted her brother, goaded out of his usual mildness. 'You speak of him as if he were still in leading-strings, Harriet, and merely caught occasionally with his fingers in the honey jar! He is two-and-twenty, and still quite without conduct!' But

Harriet, he had to remember, was unaware of their brother's losses at the gaming table only a year ago, when he had come of age and seemed to imagine that somehow that gave him the right to incur debts without number: Roland had succeeded in putting a period to this gambling tendency by threatening at the time to disown both Piers and any successive debts contracted at the tables and, more effectively, by warning him that the same intelligence would be circulated amongst the habitues of the gaming hells if any more losses were brought to his notice. This had, as far as Roland knew, set a curb on Piers' recklessness in that direction, but there was the ever-present fear that he would lapse again. In the past year his brother had contented himself with merely donating Roland's money to various crack-brained schemes and investments — that morning had unveiled yet another of them.

'I tell you this,' Roland went on, and his tone left no doubt of his sincerity, 'if he continues in this fashion he will ruin me, and that I cannot allow. I have been too soft-hearted by far with him, but I shall be compelled to disown him before long. I have no choice,' he explained as he saw Harriet's anxious face, 'for no one is so prosperous at present that they may disregard profligate expenditure. Banks are failing every day, as you well know, and even our farms are not flourishing — the income from them has fallen away alarmingly ... And if this damnable spring weather doesn't improve, matters will sink still further!' he concluded, glaring at the murky street outside.

'He will think you are ostracizing him unfairly — because of what he is,' Harriet said in a tentative manner.

'Do you imagine I am not aware of that?' Roland snapped. 'It is the prime reason I have tolerated his ramshackle ways to this degree. And he will *say* I am maltreating him, of course, but he cannot think it, I am perfectly sure of that! He must know how he has tried my patience — and my purse — over the years . . . ' He gave an odd little laugh. 'The sins of the mothers visited upon the sons,' he murmured.

'Roly! I wish you will not speak like that of mama.' But there was more weariness than outrage in her voice.

'I'm sorry. But you must own her choice of paramour was not a happy one.'

'No! I fancy Parfitt was as unlike poor dear papa as could be,' Harriet observed sadly.

'He was,' confirmed Roland, still grim-faced. 'Not that I have ever met the fellow, but his ill-famed reputation lingers yet about the clubs. Well, I do not pretend to understand female quirks and fancies but even so that particular episode in mama's life never ceases to astonish me. If it weren't for the only-too-obvious similarity between Parfitt and Piers, I would beg leave to doubt the whole unsavoury business, but Piers is *not* an Aubery — he neither looks like one nor acts like one. Besides,' he said, shrugging his broad shoulders and turning from his fruitless vigil at the window, 'everyone knew of their affair, I believe, even papa.'

'Treen maintains that after mama had borne two sets of twins — and there were none known on her side of the family — she vowed she would never risk the same thing happening again, and from that day shunned poor papa.'

'That's exactly the sort of bone-headed thing I'd expect a senile lady's maid like Treen to say, and in any event it scarcely accounts for Parfitt as a choice of lover, does it?'

'No, nothing does, of course,' agreed Harriet prosaically, 'but perhaps he had an irresistible fascination for the ladies.'

'I know nothing of that but his son certainly does have, and it must only be a matter of time before he falls into some scrape with the muslin company! Then he will, as always, expect *me* to extricate him from the hornets' nest.'

16

'Well, he has not done so yet or we should have heard about it,' Harriet said placatingly. 'If he can lay siege to an heiress with his overwhelming charm, his problems — and yours — would be at an end.'

'From the way you always fly to his defence one would suppose you were *his* twin, not mine,' he observed in rueful tones.

'I feel sorry for him, you know that, Roly. Well, imagine yourself in his shoes: the youngest and only single child in a family of twins, and of different and notorious paternity! It cannot be easy for him.'

'If I stood in his shoes I think I would feel it incumbent upon me, in view of all that, to behave impeccably.'

'But then, the tainted blood does not run in your veins, does it?'

'True.' He looked thoughtfully at his sister for a moment. 'Do you suppose then, that if Piers were ignorant of the fact he is Parfitt's son he would still behave so abominably?'

'Who can say? But always remember how much worse it would be if *he* had been the firstborn and the heir — and you the youngest son!'

'God forbid!' cried Roland. 'Well, I tell you this, it would have meant the end of the Aubery fortune unless there had been fratricide committed! And then I would have been on the nubbing cheat by this time! On the other hand,' he added more soberly, 'I could have left home and followed my inclination by buying a pair of colours years ago — a course Piers has staunchly refused to follow.'

'And put a period to your existence on the battlefield at Waterloo instead of on the gallows,' Harriet said, a glint of mischief in her grey eyes.

Roland laughed. 'By all that's wonderful, what a preposterous conversation! But I am not deceived — I know you of old, you are trying to divert me from Piers' latest rig.'

'It was such a pity he was not here to see the Miss Lamberts this morning, as he seems to have discovered a very worthy cause, for once, in their proposed school.'

'Too worthy and dull for Piers, you may be sure, or he would have been here for their visit,' Roland said drily. 'But you must see he throws me into the most abominably awkward situations! He had not so much as breathed a word to me of my generous offer to donate a hundred pounds to the setting up of their school for orphans. Luckily I am not unused to his lavish bounty on my behalf, and I hope I was able to receive the ladies without their detecting my total ignorance of their mission here.'

'Oh, I'm perfectly certain they had no suspicions on that head! You rose to the occasion magnificently, Roly, and arrived at the truth of the matter almost as soon as I did.'

'Thank you, ma'am — praise indeed,' he acknowledged, inclining his head gravely, 'although I believe my ability to read the workings of my young brother's mind was, in this case, of greater consequence than any mutual thoughts of ours!'

'I wonder what has delayed Piers?' Harriet said with genuine anxiety. 'I feel sure he would have wished to be present to receive the Miss Lamberts this morning, if only to bask in your generosity.'

'I own I entertain no such fraternal confidence. The Miss Lamberts, it is patent, have no claim to beauty, title or ten thousand a year and could therefore interest Piers not one whit — beyond a fleeting desire initially to impress them, or some onlookers, with his benevolence.'

'You are too severe on him, I'll be bound! I daresay some accident has befallen him.'

'Gammon! In my experience accidents have a habit of befalling his associates, never him! I have a mind to be hard on him this time, I may say, unless he produces a wholly plausible explanation for his remiss behaviour — and frankly I can imagine none, can you?'

Harriet bit her lip. 'No . . . I confess I can't but I daresay Piers will — '

'Oh yes,' cut in Roland, 'he has no paucity of imagination!'

'That was not what I meant to say and you know it, Roly!'

'Oh, damn the boy!' exclaimed her twin irritably, tiring of the banter. 'I have enough letters to write to occupy me for the rest of the day, on top of which Henfield is coming to see me later about the possibility of selling mineral rights at Chelbeck.'

Harriet looked up in consternation. 'Oh, not in the park! It would ruin it, surely?'

'I do not doubt it — but I refer you to Piers on the matter,' he replied austerely. 'I should scarcely have to entertain the idea but for his drain on my resources . . . Ah! and here is the culprit returned now, if I am not mistaken!'

2

The elderly Marwood landau came to rest before a house in Great Stanhope Street at precisely the same point as it had a thousand times before: the coachman was a creature of habit — like his master, Sir Ralph — and halted the chestnuts' heads not six inches from the stone water trough as on every return home.

The hood of the carriage had been closed during the short but damp journey from Somerset House due to Sir Ralph's rheumaticky condition, and his two young daughters tumbled out of the stuffy atmosphere into the air with some relief.

They were also relieved to be home again and able to discuss freely between themselves the dashing figure they had encountered at the Exhibition. Their father had made some reference during their drive to the Hon. Piers Aubery of course, but only to express his anticipation at viewing that gentleman's picture gallery, and his anxiety lest he should be a Whig. ' . . . For I should not like to fall into their company, be they never so exalted.' And by implication he meant that his daughters should not associate with any Whig either.

Sir Ralph Marwood, a high Tory gentleman, chiefly concerned with his country property in Kent, Hollsted Manor, nonetheless made an annual pilgrimage to his London house still, solely on account of his two unmarried daughters: they had not caught husbands in Hollsted and the season in Town, therefore, could not be ignored, even though there was a much greater danger there of encountering a Whig family unawares — a thing not conceivable in their native Hollsted. There, the ancestry and allegiance of every neighbouring family was known, and the sympathies and social rank of all newcomers were quickly discovered — and thus the welcome extended varied in degree from cordiality to a mere civility.

However, as far as Sir Ralph was aware, the old Lord Bittadon, although known to have been something of a philanthropist, had had no liberal Whiggish leanings, and he must hope his sons followed his lead: sons often didn't in these disordered days, though, and he would verify the matter as soon as maybe. In the meantime, he felt it would have been ill-advised of him to reject the generous, if impulsive invitation to visit Bittadon House; Emily and Sophia should be given every opportunity to make the acquaintance of suitable partis. His widowed sister, Mary Ashton, to whom his motherless daughters were now entrusted, had proved conspicuously lacking in the sort of push which was needed to launch young ladies upon the London season: she had had no daughters, only two sturdily independent sea-going sons, which left her ill-prepared for her present position.

In itself the task of finding husbands for his girls should not have proved an onerous one. They had been well-schooled by his own dear wife in every aspect of ladylike accomplishments, and by himself they were well-endowed with comfortable fortunes; and although his was a parent's partial eye he did not fancy any would disagree that they were young ladies of pleasing countenance and lively disposition — Sophia might be said to be a trifle too lively on occasions, but she would sober with time to be sure . . .

However, if he had seen her after their return home that day he might have doubted the likelihood of sobriety ever setting in. Sophia burst into the parlour, tossed off her poke bonnet revealing a mop of golden curls, danced round Mary Ashton, who was seated before the Pembroke table immersed in her work, and cried: 'We've had a capital morning, Aunt Ashton, haven't we, Emmy?'

Her precipitate appearance had quite literally set the feathers flying.

'Oh, do be careful, child!' remonstrated her aunt goodnaturedly, as she snatched at the bright floating feathers and in so doing displaced many more. She was making feather-decorated boxes — a current craze amongst ladies and initiated in the Marwood household by Sophia, with all the enthusiasm of youth.

But now that young lady said impatiently: 'Oh, pray don't waste your time on those silly things, Aunt!'

'Sophia!' her elder sister said in warning tones, 'Remember you are eighteen not eight years old! And,' she went on, helping Mrs Ashton to retrieve the feathers, '*this* was your notion in the first place. I hope you do not intend to abandon all these materials.'

'But they are not abandoned: Aunt Ashton is using them up!' Sophia pointed out saucily.

'Yes.' agreed Mary in placid accents,

'I own I have become rather fond of the occupation.'

Emily stifled the retort which had sprung to her lips, and wished her meek aunt would occasionally support her when she endeavoured to admonish Sophia: she felt she herself — at two-and-twenty — to be the guardian in the family more often than not. 'Do you sit down, Sophia,' was all she said, and even then wished she had not.

Her young sister perched on the edge of the little table, picked up the feathers one by one and blew them from the palm of her hand. Her aim, if she had one, seemed to be to lodge a feather in an empty box baldly awaiting its cladding. 'We met the most handsome man I've ever seen at the Exhibition, Aunt — Lord Bittadon's brother — and we're invited to dine on Friday — just imagine, dinner at Bittadon House in Grosvenor Street!' She imparted this knowledge between energetic puffs. 'Did you notice, Emmy, what amazing green eyes he had? — just like emeralds.'

'No, I did not, and whatever colour they are I would recommend you refrain from gazing into them in a moonstruck fashion when next you meet!'

'Bittadon,' mused Aunt Ashton, screwing up her eyes and adding several years and many wrinkles to her small pointed face. 'I do believe Bittadon was patron of the home for orphans of the sea in Shoreditch — or is it Spitalfields? My son, George, would know I expect, for he had the unpleasant task of placing a family of orphans there. One of the sailors on his ship was killed — or did he die of the fever on the way home from the Indies? No . . . I fancy it can't have been the fever for it was aboard the *Leopard* if I remember aright.'

Emily was used to the cloud of verbiage with which her aunt smothered everything, and she never found it easy to stem it without seeming incivil. It was a matter of fine timing, she had found, and now she interposed quickly: 'Yes, I'm sure that must have been the present Lord Bittadon's father: papa was telling us of his philanthropic leanings.' Emily cast a minatory look at Sophia, still blowing feathers to the winds in a bored manner.

'Oh, I'm so dizzy!' the young girl announced, taking the hint in her own fashion and sliding from the table. 'What shall I wear on Friday?' she asked, executing a few waltz steps with an invisible partner. 'Oh, do you suppose my new ball dress could be ready by then?'

'I expect so, my dear,' Mrs Ashton said, always anxious to indulge her favourite niece.

Emily thought the dress would be too showy by far for a modest dinner, even at Bittadon House — but then decided it might be a very glittering affair for all she knew about it. 'Come, Sophia, we must change at once for *today's* dinner — papa must not be kept waiting.'

There was no immediate response

from her sister, who was now leafing through the latest copy of *La Belle Assemblée* for the fashion plates, but Mrs Ashton cried: 'Oh dear, no!' and rose to her feet shaking feathers from her brown muslin skirts. 'And there is all this jumble to clear away yet,' she added with some agitation.

'Don't fret over that, Aunt,' Emily told her. 'I'll ring for Jenny.'

'Oh yes, of course.'

Mrs Ashton, accustomed to a much humbler style of life, was still unused to the army of servants which waited upon her brother and his small family. When they were resident in Great Stanhope Street, the inhabitants were outnumbered two to one by a butler, lady's maid, cook, abigail, two footmen, coachmen and two grooms: when the family removed to their country establishment, Hollsted Manor, the ratio increased to three to one, but there they were all swallowed up in the rambling Elizabethan pile and its environs. In the smaller town house the presence of so many servants was oppressive, but Mary Ashton was relieved that here, at least, her brother had the ordering of the household — in Kent it fell to her lot to supervise the Marwoods' formidable housekeeper, Mrs Young. In reality, though, Emily ensured the smooth-running of both establishments by tactful intervention when her absent-minded elders failed to give the necessary guidance.

As Emily went upstairs now, with her young sister at her side still prattling about her latest hero, she hoped Sophia would find a husband this season. However, this might not be easy as Sophia could not be thrust forward on society until she herself as the eldest daughter was at least betrothed. In a less rigid family this observance might be set aside but her father was a stickler in such matters. Moreover, until Sophia was settled, Emily did not feel able to marry and leave her father and aunt to her mercy. Not that she could deem this to be any severe imposition at the moment, as she had met no one who had claimed both her hand and her heart; several gentlemen had laid claim to the former but she had rejected them all. Sir Ralph, fortunately, although old-fashioned, was not a vindictive parent and had no wish to foist unwanted partners upon his daughters, however desirable they might be as sons-in-law.

When the girls arrived at their shared bedchamber — for rooms were scarce in a house so swarming with staff — their lady's maid, Brice, was already there to speed them on their way to the dinner-table promptly by three o'clock. Sir Ralph not only kept early country hours but early behind-the-age country hours, to which he had been accustomed in his youth.

Brice had been with the Marwood family only for three years, and was not, to Emily's regret, a faithful old retainer to whom she might have turned in times of difficulty. Their old nurse had died soon after Lady Marwood. In fact the engaging of the youngish maid had been one of Emily's first tasks after her mother's death: Aunt Ashton had been present at the interviews, of course, but the decisions had been left to Emily while her aunt talked very much off the point as always. However, the servant had proved efficient in her duties and respectful in manner, both scarce enough qualities to discover, and if she lacked sagacity and wisdom to any degree it did not set her much beneath her true employers.

In short, Emily felt that the whole burden of steering her sister safely into conformable marriage rested upon her shoulders. And there were times when she doubted her capacity to achieve this: today was one of them.

Sophia lost no time in telling Brice of her latest beau (for such he had become in her mind in the space of a few hours) — and how one dart from his peculiar and verdant eyes had quite rendered her his slave for life.

'What nonsense you do talk!' Emily

interrupted. 'I cannot vouch for the colour of the gentleman's eyes but certainly you are a *green* girl if you imagine he so much as noticed you. He struck up an acquaintanceship with papa over their mutual interest in painting, and you must not refine too much on the matter.' She was uncomfortably aware, though, that his gaze had fixed upon herself rather more than was necessary and she hoped Sophia had not noticed that circumstance. 'Besides,' she said teasingly, 'we shall no doubt encounter a Mrs Aubery on Friday — and, who knows, several infant Auberys, perhaps!'

Sophia's plump features froze in dismay, and her blue eyes rounded. 'Oh no, you cannot be serious, Emmy!'

★ ★ ★

Harriet stared at her newly-returned brother. 'You cannot be serious! Do I understand you have invited two completely chance-met ladies to dinner?

34

— on Friday!' she added, as if that made matters worse — which it did, as she had fixed for two of their close friends to take dinner with them that evening. She had not reckoned upon Piers gracing the table with his presence at all; he rarely did so on such occasions.

'Oh no,' disclaimed Piers with a bland air, 'not two, dear Harry, but three chance-met guests altogether — their father accompanies them.'

He was the only person to call her Harry and she disliked it, but it passed unnoticed at the moment. She was about to express her general outrage over the invitation when Roland, who had been seething unheard in the background ever since his brother's belated return, intervened violently. 'Piers!' he roared, causing even that young man to blanch a little, 'unless you have an exceedingly good explanation for your monstrous behaviour this morning I doubt you will be in residence under my roof by sundown tonight, let alone Friday!'

'Dash it all, Roly, that's coming it a bit strong, ain't it?' he drawled, making a quick recovery. He leaned against the sofa table, folded his arms and absently stroked a sleeve of his exquisite blue superfine coat, which had so impressed Sophia Marwood by its magnificence. 'And all because I offer hospitality to three people! No, I'll not believe you are such a scrape-penny you would begrudge a dinner to anyone.'

This generous estimate of his brother was ignored. 'Am I to understand,' Roland asked coldly, 'that an earlier invitation of yours, to the Miss Lamberts, to be precise, has escaped your memory?'

'Lambert . . . ' Piers said, withdrawing a hand from appreciation of the superfine and placing long slim fingers across his brow. 'Oh, good God yes! The two school-room antidotes!' he exclaimed, looking up with an air of achievement. 'Met them at the Wendle's jollification — can't think what the devil they were doing there, but they seemed — '

'All that concerns me,' Roland interpolated grimly, 'is that *I* met them here, this morning, and was relieved of one hundred pounds — a sum which I could ill afford, I may say. Well . . . ?'

'Well, it was a deuced good cause, if my memory serves me right — can't deny that — just the sort of thing we Auberys have supported for ever.'

Harriet, whose glance had been going from brother to brother as if she were watching a game of battledore and shuttlecock, held her breath in apprehension when she heard Piers refer to 'we Auberys': it was, she was sure, an intentional ploy of his to taunt his brother. But Roland, she would have known, would not hurl Piers' dubious ancestry in his face no matter how incensed he was.

'Setting aside the disastrous financial aspect of the affair — although God knows I must return to it soon enough — do you not think it was just a trifle remiss of you not to give me prior warning of the Miss Lamberts' call? — indeed, without wishing to overburden you with duties, might it not have been possible for you to be present yourself to receive them?' Roland said with biting sarcasm.

Piers gave an uneasy laugh. 'Had every intention of doing just that, but must have drunk the waters of Lethe, you know! Well — too much wine last night, in any event!' he finished feebly.

Harriet was conscious that her presence was unlikely to be appreciated as the fraternal dialogue became more acrimonious. 'If you will excuse me, gentlemen,' she murmured, 'I must attend to the week's menus.'

Her twin had in fact quite forgotten she was there, but was not sorry to be left alone with Piers at that point.

'Piers,' he said quietly, when the door closed, 'I do not intend to rant and rave — it is not my way — but do not be deceived by that circumstance . . . A twelve-month ago I had to warn you to curb your gambling debts — '

'Yes, dammit, and I've kept my word, haven't I?' he fired up. 'What more do you want?'

'Yes, it's true you have,' agreed Roland, determined to be scrupulously fair. 'But since then various schemes and causes, originated wholly by you, have been a constant and quite unlooked for burden on our resources. Now those resources, whatever you may think, are not limitless. The bulk of the estate is entailed and I must rely on income and rapidly diminishing investment for our support. If we are to be philanthropic I would rather have the choosing of the beneficiaries myself, and the amount of the gift — do I make myself clear?'

'But I have made good investments for you!' Piers blustered. 'Why, those paintings alone — '

'Those painting, which you kindly bought in my name at Phillips' salerooms for — if I remember aright — twenty thousand pounds, would not raise enough now to pay your tailoring bill at Schulz's for one week!'

'Oh no, you must be out, there!' Piers said decisively.

'Indeed I am not! I had them valued only last week.'

'How could you, Roly, such exquisite works of art? I selected them with the utmost discrimination so that they should enhance the family heirlooms. You have a Gothick streak in you — I have always suspected it ... In any event they are bound to come about in a year or two, mark my words.'

'I daresay, and in the meantime we shall be white-washed.' Roland was not entirely devoid of sympathy for Piers who, he thought, really did seem to imagine his efforts were of the greatest benefit to the family. Unfortunately, as he had none of the responsibility of running the estate he had little notion of the true value of money.

'What! The Auberys bankrupt! Never!' exclaimed Piers who, still propped languidly against the table, was startled into an upright posture. 'You are merely trying to frighten me.'

'Well, you have *succeeded* in frightening me,' retorted his brother bluntly.

'Sir Ralph Marwood — the gentleman I encountered at Somerset House this morning,' Piers began quickly, creating a diversion, 'is desirous of seeing our paintings — and he's a well-blunted cove with a discerning eye if ever I saw one.'

'In which case he'll have more sense than to part company with more than a handful of guineas for those canvases,' Roland countered in brusque tones.

'I was wondering.' Piers reflected airily, and as if none of the earlier conversation had taken place, 'if I might not take a tour of the continent. I was deprived of the Grand Tour, as you know, because of Boney's damned war . . . '

And thank God for it, thought Roland for the hundredth time, well aware what such a tour might have cost

41

the family in lost reputation and gained *objets d'art.*

'... but now the whole world is in Paris,' Piers concluded blithely.

'By all means, I should not stand in your way — indeed, could not. You are of age — and responsible for your own affairs.'

'Living is a deal cheaper across the Channel, I collect, so I daresay I could keep the wolf from the door for say ...' He raised his eyes in contemplation to the crystal chandelier — which evidently served to inflate his ideas. '... two thousand a year.'

'The I recommend you stay where you are. Your allowance is one thousand pounds, if you remember.'

Piers had been prepared to haggle, hence the optimistic starting figure, and also he fancied that his brother might leap at the idea of his leaving the country. 'But you said — '

'I said you were free to go to Paris or anywhere else. I did not say I would frank your foreign escapades; anymore than I will frank your home-brewed ones, as from today.'

A look of incredulity greeted this statement. Piers, who had been pacing the floor, was only a few feet from his brother who seemed to tower over him. 'You expect me to manage on a thousand pounds?'

'For the moment, yes — but you may have to contrive on less if matters don't improve on the estates.' Before Piers had chance to recover from this blow, Roland delivered another one. 'You could always earn your living,' he suggested.

The younger man gasped like a landed fish for a moment, then cried in aggrieved tones: 'But I have tried! And you would not countenance it!'

Roland looked blankly at his brother, then his brow cleared. 'Oh, you mean that absurd notion you had of setting up a pugilistic club, and flying in the face of Gentleman Jackson!'

'It was not absurd! And had you not cavilled about a paltry loan for the premises, even now I should be proprietor of the most prosperous sparring school in town — and plagued by none of these petty considerations of money!' he added for good measure.

'Come, Piers! Unless Jackson had died laughing at your effrontery in putting up in opposition to him with a bruiser, whose only commendation was that he had gone ten rounds once with Mendoza — who was well past his best at the time — then I fear your chances of success were faint indeed! No,' Roland said firmly, 'I was referring to a profession — the army, I know, is not for you, nor the church, but I can see no reason why you should not apply yourself to the study of the law. You fared well enough at Oxford . . . '

'Good God, no! Can you see me in black fustian and a bag-wig or whatever those legal coves wear?'

It was difficult to do so, certainly, but Roland felt disinclined to treat the matter so lightly. 'If you are quite determined to set your face against a profession then I can only give you due warning that you must live within your means, or you might find yourself on the wrong side of the law, perhaps.'

'How so?' Piers narrowed his eyes, which were more of a glaucous shade than the emerald glint the romantically-minded Sophia had attributed to them. 'Oh, you mean blown up at point nonplus and landing in the Fleet . . . You wouldn't let it happen, Roly,' he said quietly.

'Do not depend on it,' was the even softer reply.

3

The weather continued wet and cold, as it had throughout the spring, and by the time the day of the dinner at Bittadon House arrived only one of the protagonists viewed it with anything approaching buoyant spirits — and that was Piers, who had quite decided the event would mark the beginning of a change for the better in his fortunes. As for the rest of the host family, Harriet was still nurturing a grievance against the three interlopers — as she saw them — thrust on to her small dinner-party by Piers; Roland, apart from an understandable caution about his young brother's acquaintance, also resented the fact that he had to suffer the intrusion of these strangers at his table, when he had hoped to approach one of their own guests upon a very delicate family matter some time during the evening.

The Marwoods were also, for various reasons, unenthusiastic about the pending arrangement. Sir Ralph had been severely afflicted with the rheumatics of late and would not have contemplated the shortest drive in such inclement weather had he not considered the connexion with the Aubery family one of promise for his daughters. Emily also feared for her father's health in being exposed to the damp for even the briefest space, and in addition was becoming more apprehensive than ever over her sister's possible outrageous behaviour at Bittadon House: she even wished Aunt Ashton was to accompany them to keep a curb on Sophia, ineffective though her aunt's influence might be. Sophia's enthusiasm for dining at her beau's table was undampened by weather or any outside consideration, but she had thrown out a spot on her cheek and it looked like reaching its zenith on Friday: this circumstance, coupled with the fact that her ball dress would not be completed in time, sunk her into such a crotchety state Emily began to wonder if it wouldn't be better to cry off altogether. However, Aunt Ashton, galvanized by a serious suggestion from Sophia that a beauty patch was all that was needed to disguise her blemish, set to with a will to obliterate the offending spot by more acceptable means.

When the Marwood family was finally ready to leave for Grosvenor Street, Emily suspected her sister might be wearing a hint of rouge although she was in such a high state of excitement it was impossible to tell. Whatever her methods, Emily had to admit Aunt Ashton had made Sophia, always angelic-looking in white, appear as fetching as she had ever seen her. She hoped sincerely there *was* a Mrs Aubery to temper her sister's rapture . . .

On arrival at Bittadon House, after they had ascended the splendidly curving marble stair at a suitably unhurried pace to accommodate Sir Ralph's infirmity, they were announced, and Emily found herself face to face with their hostess. For a fleeting moment she thought her hope had been fulfilled and that this was indeed Mrs Aubery. Judging by Sophia's stricken look she had leapt to the same conclusion, but it was quickly made plain that although there was little facial resemblance they were speaking to a sister of the gentleman who had issued their invitation.

Harriet, steeled for the worst where Piers' choice of casual acquaintance was concerned, was pleasantly surprised at the Marwoods: the father impressed her with his courteous manner and bearing although it was apparent to her that he was suffering not a little from his crippling condition: the two daughters, from her own mature viewpoint of eight-and-twenty years, struck her as very pretty young creatures with blue eyes, glowing complexions and fair hair. If, as Piers had been hinting all week, these young ladies were heiresses, perhaps he would solve all their problems by marrying one of them: for Harriet, much in the way of Emily Marwood, had been inclined to postpone her own nuptials until such time as the youngest member of the family was safely settled. Although in her case the matter was complicated by two factors; firstly, she was a little reluctant to leave her twin, Roland, and secondly, she could not be said to be violently in love with her suitor of long-standing, Ned Grimsby.

Nonetheless, when that gentleman arrived a moment later, they greeted each other with an ease of familiarity which spoke of a firm friendship.

In due time Emily and Sophia had met and spoken with all their fellows in the vast reception room, and Emily was relieved to see that it was to be a modest gathering, for Lord Bittadon's twin sister, Harriet, had pronounced everyone to be present after Mr Grimsby's arrival with his mother. In this estimation, thought Emily, she must have ignored her brother, as Piers Aubery had not yet made his appearance. Until he should arrive, Sir Ralph had been settled by the fire with great solicitude by Harriet and was now in earnest converse with Lord Bittadon. Emily and her young sister had been taken under the wing of an Aubery aunt, Mrs Knowle, who proved a forthright and ebullient lady.

'You must be wondering, I daresay, what an old Tough like me is doing at a gathering of young people.'

Emily smiled uncertainly at this prelude for such a sentiment had never crossed her mind, but Mrs Knowle went on:

'Harriet is a real out-and-outer, a splendid gel, always invites her old Aunt to a neat dinner whenever she can. Not that you would fancy I stood in need of one, eh?' she chuckled, and patted with her fan a broad expanse of taut violet satin under a matching shelf-like bosom. 'Of course I am only asked when there are no niffy fellow guests who might take huff at my vulgar ways!' she confided in a sonorous whisper to the two girls, who watched the nodding ostrich feather on her head in fascination. 'Oh pray, do not misunderstand me, I did not mean to imply that *you* are not the most well-bred gels imaginable — but you have a sense of humour, I can see that by the twinkle in those lovely blue eyes! Greatest asset there is, believe me!'

Emily wondered how this astonishing lady would impress her staid papa, and found herself at a loss as to how to reply to these startling observations. However, a diversion was created as Piers made a belated entrance then, and after a pause to survey the assembled company and a brief internal battle as to whether to approach Sir Ralph — who was with Roly, his elder brother — or the two daughters — who were with his formidable and distressing aunt — he came down in favour of interrupting the latter group: it would not do for the Marwood ladies to be given a disgust of the family before he had even had time to woo one of them.

When he came into the room Emily thought he was the only gentleman there who seemed to accord with the rich and ornate Louis Quatorze setting. His fellows were in sober evening coats, black breeches and white silk stockings which looked stark indeed against the gilded Boulle furniture, Aubusson carpet and aqueous green silk drapes but he, it seemed, had dressed with the background in mind — which he had, of course, although carefully modified so as not to offend the sensibilities of the old gentleman whose good opinion was essential for his plans. Consequently the sage green striped velvet coat had been set aside for a plain cloth one only a shade lighter than the conformable olive, the waistcoat was green and white with horizontal stripes, and the breeches a delicate green; the whole effect in Emily's eyes a trifle dandyish for her taste but Sophia could find no fault in it.

He gave a repressive nod to his Aunt Knowle, then made his bow to the sisters and greeted them like long lost friends. ' . . . I own I was afraid you might not come after all, and I would have been quite desolated if you had not.'

'Oh, but we would not have missed the opportunity of seeing your picture collection for the world, would we, Sophia?' Emily replied in dampening tones to this over-effusive welcome, and brought a glint of amusement to Mrs Knowle's dark eyes.

'Ah yes, but that was the trouble!' Piers cried undeterred. 'You had only a few dreary canvases to lure you here, whilst I had the prospect of the company of two of the most beautiful young ladies in town! It is scarcely a fair exchange, I know it.'

Sophia accepted this as her due and smiled complacently: Emily would have made a more spirited response but was forestalled.

'A tongue steeped in the syrup of ambrosia, as always, eh?' intervened his aunt in chaffing tones. 'Well, you'll not flummery these two gels! They're wide awake upon every suit, mark my words.' She looked indulgently at her young companions and said: 'Yes, I can leave you quite safely, I'm sure, with this fribble of a nephew of mine. I must go and pay my respects to Bittadon as he is paying for my dinner!'

Emily wished she felt as confident of Sophia's good sense as did this lady who spoke in cant like a man. She was almost sorry for the discomfited nephew until, that is, he said:

'Touched in the upper-works, you know, there's no help for it, but I wish my sister wouldn't invite her — gives the family a bad name . . . Well, shall we view the picture gallery before dinner? There is an hour at our disposal.'

'We should be delighted, of course, but I'm not altogether sure of papa's wishes in the matter — he may prefer to

wait until after we have dined,' Emily
told him.

'Oh, he will indeed!' giggled Sophia.
'Papa will be as cross as crabs to be
kept from his dinner until six o'clock.'

'Sophia!' said Emily in scandalized
tones; but Piers was all solicitude.

'Then I'm sure we cannot allow that,'
he said at once. 'Sir Ralph is accustomed to dine early, I collect?'

'Oh yes, we are monstrously countri-
fied and always dine at three! Just
fancy!' Sophia obligingly informed him.

Warning looks and chiding words
were of no avail to restrain her sister, as
Emily knew; and short of muzzling her
there seemed no solution to be had, she
thought, as she watched helplessly while
Piers Aubery hastened to the fireside
where his sister was lending a solicitous
ear to their father.

'Really Sophia,' Emily could not help
saying, 'I wish you will think a little
before you speak.'

'Mm?' was the abstracted response,
as Sophia gazed dreamily at Piers

across the room. 'Why, what have I done wrong? Papa is always out of reason cross if his dinner is delayed.'

'Scarcely when he is in someone else's house! Unlike you he has some notion of how to conduct himself . . . '

But the conversation at the hearth intruded at this point.

' . . . I expect you favour an early dinner, as I do, sir. Yes, well, we always dine at five here, you know! Harry, you will ring right away, won't you?' Piers asked in his beautifully modulated voice. 'Peck is a little late, I do believe.'

Even at some yards distance, Emily saw his sister bite back a retort, but an angry flush she could not control so easily.

'Oh . . . yes, of course,' she responded, and recovering sufficiently to smile reassuringly at her uncomfortable guest, Sir Ralph, who she sensed would be the last person in the world to cause embarrassment to his hostess. 'But I daresay there has been some unavoidable delay in the kitchens.'

Emily saw Lord Bittadon turn away from Mrs Knowle and scowl ferociously at his young brother: she was rather startled by this glare for she had thought him a gentle-natured person when they met earlier.

'There now,' she murmured to Sophia, 'you may see the trouble you have caused! I daresay the cook may storm out now and we shall have no dinner at all.'

But Sophia had not really been listening to the exchange by the fire, and as Ned Grimsby approached them at that moment she was spared an answer.

'Piers is setting the cat among the pigeons as always, I see!' he said with an easy smile. 'But then, if you are particular friends of his I must be careful what I say, must I not?'

Mr Grimsby had already been briefly presented to them but Emily took the opportunity now to study him more closely. She saw a lean, brown-faced, brown-eyed man of medium height; he was, she supposed, about thirty and had a rather erect military bearing about him. A sharper contrast with the effusive and elegant Piers could not be imagined than this forthright-looking, plainly attired man. She guessed at once he did not like Piers.

'Oh no, we cannot claim a particular friendship, or indeed a friendship at all, for we only met a few days ago — when he very kindly invited papa to see his picture gallery — and here we are!'

'Oh yes, the picture gallery,' said Mr Grimsby in a knowing voice, and still smiling. But then he seemed to recollect that his audience was two strange young ladies not as familiar with Piers' ways as he was. 'You are interested in painting, then?'

'Papa and I are; Sophia prefers the more animated art of music-making,' Emily explained.

'Ah, then I daresay we can look forward to hearing some duets before long for I must own Piers has a splendid singing voice,' he said magnanimously.

'I should so like to hear him,' Sophia breathed.

'You will, never fear,' Ned Grimsby assured her, his magnanimity fading in spite of himself. ' . . . But not yet awhile, for here is Peck to announce dinner, if I am not mistaken. Poor fellow, he looks as though he has had to put down a riot in the kitchen!' he chuckled.

Piers advanced towards them to claim the honour of leading Emily into dinner: Ned Grimsby hastened away to Harriet's side for he always partnered her: Sir Ralph was escorting the petite sprightly widow, Mrs Grimsby: Roland took young Miss Sophia Marwood's elbow as it became clear she fell to his responsibility to hand into dinner; and Mrs Knowle stood apart from this pairing off cermony, and said in a penetratingly cheerful voice:

'Don't fret about me, Harriet dear, I can find my own way to the table after all these years! Still, I give you due warning, as you haven't provided a partner for me I may take revenge by eating enough for two!'

'She always does,' muttered Piers to himself.

Roland took his place at the head of the table and tried not to catch his twin's eye at the foot, for he felt sure she must be finding the gathering every bit as tedious as he was, in addition to her natural apprehensions about what was to be served for this unexpectedly early repast. Not that he had expected to enjoy himself, but as the meal progressed it seemed to him that a dreary occasion was turning into a disaster. Sophia Marwood, at his right, was as tongue-tied as she was pretty, he discovered, although Piers, on her other hand, soon had her chattering like a magpie. Indeed, in his preoccupation with Sophia, Piers neglected the partner of his own choosing, Emily, who in turn seemed to be attracting Ned Grimsby's earnest attention.

This latter circumstance disturbed Roland more than anything else, and whilst keeping up a lively dialogue with his garrulous Aunt Knowle, at his left — not a difficult feat, luckily, and one to which he was well accustomed — he cursed Piers afresh to himself for spoiling what had been planned as a small private party. Harriet originally had invited only Ned and his mother. For although Harriet had turned down Ned's offer of marriage some years before, the Grimsbys had remained close friends of the Auberys. Ned had proposed when he had been home on leave from the Peninsula three years ago — he had just been made Brigade-major — and as he was going back to join the thick of the battle again neither he (nor Roland) had scarcely been surprised that Harriet should demur a little about marriage.

However, Ned had sold out after Waterloo and was now established as a country gentleman at his late father's estate not ten miles from Chelbeck

— the Aubery family seat in Northamptonshire. Harriet and Ned had met at a local assembly in the county five years before, and Roland's attitude to a possible match between them had been a divided one at the time: he felt that Ned would make an admirable husband for his twin but could not disregard the fact that he was an army officer engaged in service overseas; and, more selfishly, Roland relied on Harriet to preside over the Chelbeck domestic arrangements and act hostess for him. The latter circumstance they had both expected to be temporary until he should himself marry.

But matters had not fallen out that way and Roland was beginning to feel anxious on his twin's behalf: he had no wish to see her dwindle into a spinster — she had already taken to wearing a cap, which was a lowering enough step for his taste, and one which he deplored — and that night he had resolved to have a word in Ned's ear. It would have been a deuced ticklish subject to broach, and he had not the smallest desire to act matchmaker or interfere in his sister's affairs — which at twenty-eight she was more than capable of managing for herself — but he did have a suspicion that her reservations in the matter could be overcome, if Ned were to renew his suit with a shade more dash . . .

However, as Roland cast an eye gloomily around his table and observed Ned applying all the dash in the world to conversing, nay flirting with his neighbour, Miss Marwood, he did not know whether to be sorry or glad he had been prevented from approaching him that evening. Harriet was left to talk with Sir Ralph and Mrs Grimsby and was doing it with her usual warmth and amiability — and if she noticed Ned's neglect of her, as she must, she gave no sign of it. (In fact, her present anxieties were all directed towards the precipitate dinner and whether cook would be able to dress enough dishes to send to the table.) Piers, he noticed, was still monopolizing Sophia Marwood — or perhaps she was monopolizing him, it was hard to tell: she seemed a determined young woman and was clearly quite besotted with his wretched brother already. Roland did try drawing her attention from him briefly, but again she lapsed into a silence as complete as her previous animation, so he abandoned her to Piers. After all, he reflected, if Piers was succeeding in fixing the interest of even a minor heiress why should he interfere in that possibility?

Although, to the casual eye, the company was a congenial and cheerful enough gathering Roland was not sorry when Harriet led away the ladies. He glanced at the remaining gentlemen around the table and thought what a disparate trio they were: Sir Ralph, who looked rather a formidable old man, glaring at all and sundry from under his bushy brows — although Roland gradually realized this was the result of short sight rather than short temper;

Ned Grimsby, whose dark features in repose looked a trifle solemn, and in conjunction with the upright carriage of his head, gave him too a stern aspect — which was wholly misleading, as anyone who had seen his sudden, transforming smile knew well; and Piers, who to Roly's presently jaundiced eye looked damned near being a man-milliner, set as he was between his two worthy-looking companions — but that was an unfair judgement, he knew, and merely reflected his current annoyance with his young brother.

Sir Ralph, Roland and Ned were all, in spite of being fixed in town at the moment, country gentlemen at heart, and in no time they were united in deploring the calamitous weather which had been experienced of late throughout the land. The state of the Northamptonshire acres and those of Kent were compared, the tardy crop-sowing in the cold water-logged ground lamented, as were the numbers of lambs lost in the raw spring. Each man, regardless of the trust he placed in his bailiff, was anxious about his estate, and would be easier in his mind when he could quit town and return to his native county later in the year.

It was hardly surprising if Piers, who had no rolling acres to return to, or farm rents to diminish, should find this talk a dead-bore: he decided to enliven the doom-laden rustic atmosphere.

'Dammit, if things are so parlous I can't see why you don't quit these sodden shores altogether! Follow Byron's lead, depart for warmer climes! There's a deal of sense in it, you must own!'

At mention of the notorious Lord Byron (who had of late reviled his wife publicly, had been reviled himself in a novel by his mistress, and had had an execution in his house) Sir Ralph's stare fixed balefully upon his young friend; Ned looked unamused; and Roland said drily:

'I suspect that gentleman had more pressing reasons for his departure than considerations of climate.'

'Do I take it, sir, that you hold similar views to those of Lord Byron?' Sir Ralph asked Piers with some alarm.

Piers had quite forgotten in his irritation that he should be impressing Sir Ralph with his supereminent worth as a future son-in-law, and hastened to rectify to lapse. 'Indeed not, no, how could anyone?' he replied in suitably appalled tones.

'Ah! So you wouldn't be a Whig, then?' pursued Sir Ralph eagerly.

Roland was hard put to it at this point to preserve his countenance: Piers, he knew, had not the least notion of politics and was probably completely unaware that Byron *was* a Whig. Sir Ralph, on the other hand, seemed to be unacquainted with — or untroubled by — all Byron's indiscretions except his political one.

'Whig?' echoed Piers faintly, baffled by the sudden turn in the conversation. 'No, certainly I'm not,' he said with truth.

'Capital, capital,' clucked Sir Ralph to himself. 'Oh — ' he said, remembering his host suddenly, ' — I trust I do not offend your convictions, my lord?'

'No, you'll not step on any Whiggish toes in this house! Aunt Knowle might raise her formidable voice in their support occasionally but that is merely to provoke me if she thinks I am considering speaking in the House on any Tory matter.'

Sir Ralph was well satisfied with this and required no further proof of the soundness of the Aubery family.

Piers, puzzled by the exchange, put forward the suggestion that he might conduct Sir Ralph to the picture gallery before the tea tray was carried into the drawing-room.

Roland then proposed to Ned that they rejoin the ladies, even though he could have taken that opportunity for his tête-à-tête with him instead: he felt he wanted to observe how Ned's admiration of Miss Marwood flourished before he broached the matter of his marrying Harriet . . .

Harriet and the Marwood sisters, meanwhile, had taken each other in great liking, and whilst Sophia's partiality to everything and everyone connected with the Auberys sprang from her doting upon Piers, both Emily and Harriet genuinely admired the other's good understanding and lively disposition. Harriet had soon realized that though the sisters might share the same colouring they were quite dissimilar in character, and she thought Emily surprisingly mature in outlook for one of only two-and-twenty. But as they talked she discovered that, like herself, Emily had been thrust into her mother's place at an early age — and had taken her responsibilities very seriously. Also, after only an hour or two of young Sophia's rather overwrought company, she could see that Miss Marwood had her problems. At least she had not had to fret about Piers' conduct in the same way, Harriet reflected thankfully;

she left that to Roly.

Emily, for her part, was delighted they had come to Bittadon House. She was much struck with Harriet's good sense and only regretted they had not met sooner — she had lacked companionship of a friend of a similar age and disposition. She liked Mrs Grimsby, too, with her bird-like liveliness, and her son Ned. Emily had been very flattered he should pay her such attention and make her feel almost like an old friend in the strange company: no such effort had been made by Lord Bittadon, whose house it was, but she thought him a trifle distant and rather given to casting black looks about him. It was hard to think of him as the twin of the warm-hearted amiable Harriet. Finally, the Auberys' blatant and outspoken Aunt Knowle, although alarming on first acquaintance, seemed quite well-disposed and was a refreshing change from most aunts she had met.

Emily and Harriet were deep in

conversation like two matrons about the difficulties of hiring and keeping servants — the earlier debacle in the kitchen being unmentioned but understood between them — when Sir Ralph and Piers returned to enquire if Emily and Sophia wished to accompany them to the gallery. Sophia was on her feet at once and tripping to Piers' side, and Emily, who really did want to see the paintings, followed her.

There were not above twenty canvases on the walls but, as Sir Ralph commented, they were all gems of their kind: they were mostly landscapes — and scenes by Poussin, Claude Lorrain and Guardi particularly took Sir Ralph's eye.

'You must be proud to be the owner of such a magnificent collection — I commend your taste, sir; and envy your possession of them, although I should not say so.'

Piers grasped at this polite encomium: if he could sell the whole to Sir Ralph it would, in one stroke, re-instate him with Roly, and incline Sir Ralph to look upon him with favour for such a sacrificial gesture. 'Indeed, I am deeply touched you should view them with such veneration, sir. In the ordinary way I should not bear to contemplate parting with a single one of them, of course,' he said with a sweeping gesture, 'but I can see you are a connoisseur of the highest integrity, and for you alone I could endure making an exception.'

Sir Ralph transferred his gaze from the Guardi, snatched off his spectacles and looked under bristling brows at Piers. 'Oh dear, no, sir!' he protested. 'I would not dream of inflicting such a deprivation on anyone. I know what years of devoted search and selection must go into the acquisition of such prizes.' He seemed to have overlooked the youth of the collector concerned, but nevertheless a shade more devotion could have gone into their acquisition than was in fact the case: Piers had bought them all as one lot on a mischance — he had been playing the great art collector that day to impress some friend or other, he had forgotten why, and had fully expected to be outbid. Hence the usual necessity to give his brother's name for the purchase . . .

'That is true, of course . . . ' Piers agreed, a distracted look coming into his grey-green eyes, whilst he tried to think of a way of persuading Sir Ralph to overcome his scruples.

However, Sophia, who could not bear to see such anguish afflict her idol, burst out passionately: 'You could not do it, papa! It would not be right at any price!'

'Very true, my dear,' her father acknowledged mildly, 'although I own I was tempted if only for a moment!'

Piers, who by this time had decided upon fixing the interest of the elder Miss Marwood — for the practical reasons that she was already of age and liable to be in possession of any fortune, as well as being clearly a more reasonable and silent female than the young sister — glared balefully at the confused Sophia for a moment. Then, seeing no help for it, put on a good face.

'Yes, you are in the right of it — I should be dreadfully cut up if I had to part with any of my treasures.' He could at least display a sensitive nature ... and a generous one, he decided. 'But whenever you care to, sir, I wish you will come to see them, and you Miss Marwood,' he concluded, bestowing one of his most charming smiles on Emily.

They discussed the merits of the paintings and once again that evening Emily was surprised and flattered at the attention she received from a gentleman. Nor was this the end of it, for by the time the party returned to the drawing-room to drink tea Ned Grimsby had evidently been busy: Mrs Grimsby invited the Marwood girls to a small gathering of young people she was planning in the next week or two.

'We should like it of all things, of course, but I should explain Sophia is not yet out and I'm not sure she should attend.'

'It will be the most informal affair, I do assure you, Miss Marwood, and you need have no qualms on that head.'

So, but not without a good many qualms, Emily accepted for them both; Aunt Ashton should chaperon them on that occasion, she decided, if only to attempt to impose some restraint on Sophia's flirtatious tendencies towards Piers — who had made sure he was invited, too.

Harriet was a silent onlooker to this arrangement. Although she had taken Emily in great liking, she could scarcely welcome Ned's obvious attentiveness to her and was rather surprised to find how jealous she was; nor could she derive any comfort from Piers' equally evident interest in the same lady, for Sir Ralph would surely never let his daughter marry Piers — he would recognize him for the fortune-hunter she had to admit he was — and that suggested Ned's suit might be the successful one.

4

'I do believe you bother your head quite unnecessarily about things, you know,' Mrs Ashton said vaguely to her niece, several days after the Bittadon House visit.

Both ladies were sewing, and Emily did not look up but asked patiently: 'What things, aunt?'

'Well, it is quite plain to me that you are getting into a prodigious pucker over this forthcoming entertainment at the . . . Gooles, is it? No! I remember — Grimsbys! I say Goole, I expect, because Mr Ashton and I spent a simply dreadful week at Goole. It rained every day, just as it is at the moment — now why was that do you suppose?' She raised her eyes briefly from the tambour-frame and blinked, then she laughed. 'Oh, I don't mean why did it *rain*, but why were we in

Goole? It must have been in '95, I think — '

'I really could not say!' Emily cut in in desperation. 'But can *you* tell me why I worry unnecessarily?'

'Oh, so you agree with me that you do fret without cause.'

'No, I believe I have every cause,' retorted Emily, more exasperated by her aunt's diffuse manner of speaking than usual, 'but pray tell me why you think I need not be apprehensive about our visit to the Grimsbys.'

'Why, it seems to me to be perfectly admirable in every respect: a small informal gathering which Sophia can attend — and we have not had many invitations of that nature to please the dear child, have we? Without exception they are grand affairs which she must forego. I do wish your papa had let her be presented this season.'

'But she's barely eighteen,' protested Emily, although she was doubtful that Sophia's behaviour could be much more forward than it was already, in any event.

'Yes, and *you* must be allowed to take precedence for a little while longer, I know.' She stopped her fine stitchery abruptly. 'What was I saying which led to all this?'

Emily was sorely tempted to let the subject lapse but resisted. 'Our invitation to the Grimsby dance.'

'Of course! Well — aside from the fact it will be everything desirable for Sophia — I fancy from what you tell me, this Mr Grimsby is very anxious to further his acquaintance with you. And I must say he sounds quite the most eligible gentleman we have encountered this year.'

'I would advise you defer your raptures until you *have* encountered him!' Emily laughed. 'But my apprehensions concern not the Grimsbys but the Auberys — the Hon. Piers, to be exact.'

'Oh, but your papa speaks so highly of him! Indeed, I have rarely heard him so loud in his approbation — not since we met Lord . . . '

Whilst her aunt paused to recall the favoured nobleman's name, Emily said: 'Yes, I own I am at a loss to understand it but I wish he would not sing his praises in front of Sophia. She has such an impressible and ardent mind.'

'I hope you do not suggest my brother is a poor judge of character,' Mrs Ashton responded with sudden pique.

'In general, no, but I can only say I have misgivings about his estimation in this instance.' However, Emily suspected that Aunt Ashton, who had neither sisters nor daughters, was inclined by years of habit to accept masculine word as immutable law.

'You must not set yourself above your papa in these matters — it would not serve,' came the predictable response.

It was clear to Emily she would have no support in her efforts to depress Sophia's propensity to flirt with Piers, and perhaps it *was* best to ignore it.

True, he had shown no especial interest in her young sister: and she hoped his manner towards them both, which lacked the reserve and caution of most newly-met gentlemen, was merely his customary demeanour towards the opposite sex . . .

That this was so, seemed to be established beyond doubt at the Grimsbys' entertainment. It was, as Mrs Grimsby promised, a small gathering and not above eight couples took the floor for the dancing. However, Sophia's engagements in the past two weeks had been limited to morning dances — monstrously tame affairs for novices — and she was wide-eyed with excitement at being able to spread her wings at a real dance, however modest.

Mrs Ashton, after meeting their hosts and the three Auberys, expressed herself equally well-satisfied with all. 'I cannot think what you can find to criticize in any of them. The young brother I consider most engaging and quite charming. I should feel I was failing in my duty if I should put any obstacle in the way of Sophia, or you, forming an attachment there. I'm not sure I care for his sidewhiskers, but that is scarcely a circumstance of great moment!'

Mercifully, thought Emily, her sister was some distance away, talking with Harriet and her twin at the time.

' . . . Now that young man I could not like,' went on Mrs Ashton, nodding over her fan in the direction of a decidedly over-dressed youth. 'He is, I fancy, what George would call a Jessamy.'

Emily had to admit that by comparison Piers did look to be attired in no more than exquisite and expensive dress of impeccable taste.

In fact as the evening progressed Emily found she had to revise her opinions regarding several of her fellows, and mostly for the better. Sophia afforded her the most surprise and relief by behaving just as she ought. They were all, as Ned had forecast at their first meeting, favoured with a musical performance from Piers; who tried initially to persuade Emily to accompany him in his song, unaware of her lack of talent in that direction, but he seemed just as pleased when Sophia did so instead. The resultant duets were, by common consent, a remarkable achievement as the pair had had no prior rehearsal. Emily was impressed by her sister's manner, which was quite unmarred by false modesty — or by making sheep's eyes at her partner all the while.

When their cards were marked up for the dancing neither Piers nor Ned singled out any lady for his particular attention — not even herself on this occasion which, contrarily, miffed her a little.

Her final reversal of opinion concerned Lord Bittadon, who was now as good-natured as his twin and had quite lost the rather forbidding cross-grained look he had worn on their first meeting. She had an opportunity to talk with him after the completion of the quadrille, as he was leading her off the modest area of floor which Mrs Grimsby had had cleared for the dancing.

'You dance very well, Miss Marwood,' Roland told her above the general hubbub which prevailed when the trio stopped playing.

'Thank you, my lord. I am influenced by the excellence of my partners tonight, I daresay! They have, without exception, displayed a degree of skill not ordinarily encountered beyond Almack's.'

'Praise indeed! But any skill I may have is born of necessity rather than natural bent — I could not afford, with my weighty frame, to place my feet carelessly! No, my brother Piers is by far the best dancer in the family: he has an intrinsic grace in the art — and a spare form to go with it.'

'He seems a gentleman of many talents, for he has a most pleasing voice as well.'

'Oh, he is! He quite outshines me and makes me feel a veritable rustic clod on occasion!' But Roland said this in a light-hearted fashion which suggested he was not cast down by it.

Emily was a little surprised at this fraternal praise when she recalled the scowls which had been bestowed upon the same young man at their earlier meeting: but perhaps, she thought, there had been some temporary discord between them at the time.

Roland had indeed decided to call a truce after that unfortunate dinner, if Piers behaved himself in the future: for it seemed to him that many benefits would accrue if he were to be persuaded to marry one of the Marwood girls — preferably the elder sister. For she was already out and was almost bound to be possessed of a substantial endowment. In addition to which there was the consideration — which Roland knew should not have influenced him, but nonetheless it did — that it would remove Miss Marwood from Ned's reach if he were thinking of transferring his affections from Harriet. He salved his conscience by telling himself that if Ned really loved the girl he would presumably act rather more quickly in this instance than he had over Harriet, and thus cut out Piers at the start. However, he could not believe his impulsive brother would let matters hang in the hedge too long himself: the combination of an attractive female and a fortune, together with an apparently approving parent, was too good to be missed, and Piers, he hazarded, would not miss it.

Emily was quite sorry when Ned Grimsby came to claim the next dance and her enjoyable discourse with Lord Bittadon was interrupted. She thought she detected a certain annoyance on his lordship's part, also, and was mildly flattered. He, however, was only momentarily reluctant to see Ned carrying Miss Marwood away, and he realised at once the foolishness of even this: he could scarcely prevent them associating with each other so that his brother's suit might prosper!

As the gavotte proceeded Emily discovered Ned to be another partner with a high proficiency in dancing; albeit with a shade more military precision to his performance than Piers' fluent style. Before the lively dance had quite robbed Ned of his breath he asked Emily if she and her sister would care to take a drive in the park with him one morning. Emily liked Ned and accepted the offer happily, but it was not until later, when Mrs Ashton made much of the invitation, that she wondered if there was more in his attentiveness than mere punctilio.

All in all it was a successful evening, and as it was gone midnight when they left the Grimsbys' residence even Sophia was content: she had distinguished herself by singing with Piers; her new dress of white tulle over satin had been lavishly praised — by Piers; and she had danced every single dance — one of them with Piers, which was the most she had allowed herself to expect.

Emily let her sister's excited chatter flow over her and did not depress her enthusiasm for the young Aubery brother, any more than Mrs Ashton did: Sophia and Piers had both behaved unexceptionably that evening, and any fears she had had on that head were lulled for the moment.

⋆　⋆　⋆

Nothing would satisfy Mrs Ashton after this event until she had got up a dance at Great Stanhope Street to repay the hospitality they had received, and to further the relationship between the Auberys and the Marwoods: a matter which quite dominated all her thoughts these days, as much as it did Sophia's.

'I feel it in my bones, you know,' Mrs Ashton confided somewhat rashly to her nieces one day, 'that one of you is destined to be Mrs Aubery. I had exactly the same sensation, I remember, just before cousin Amelia . . . '

'Oh, aunt, do you really think so?' cried Sophia, blushing strongly as she always did at mention of the magic name.

'I said *one* of you! You cannot both have that honour,' protested Mrs Ashton with an arch smile.

'Well, you may rest assured it will not be me, for I would not accept him!' retorted Emily, as she wrote cards for the ball: Mrs Ashton had not progressed beyond putting forth the idea for the dance — Emily was left to bring it into being.

'No, of course you would not — the dark and dashing Mr Grimsby must have caught *your* interest! He is quite captivated by you, depend upon it,' said the unabashed matchmaker. 'He does so put me in mind of Sir William Kingsley, you know . . . As he was thirty years past, to be sure, so you wouldn't . . . '

Before Emily was able to curtail her aunt's ramblings, Sophia intervened.

'Then it *must* be me! *Mrs Aubery* ... .' she sighed, drawing the conversation back to her favourite topic, and abandoning all pretence of advancing her embroidery. 'But there, *I* have known it for ever!'

'Do you come off your high ropes, miss, please! I am not at all sure that papa would consent to the match, in any event, and you are still under age, remember!' But Emily knew there was no way now to undo the damage done by Aunt Ashton's thoughtless prophecy.

'Papa likes him, I know he does!'

'Yes, Emily, you must know he does, for he speaks of him in the warmest terms,' Mrs Ashton ran on quite oblivious of Emily's glance of censure. 'And someone else he speaks very highly of is a Mrs Knowle,' she said, flying off on one of her tangents. 'Another Aubery connexion, I believe. Ralph said she — '

'*Mrs Knowle!*' Emily was wholly diverted by this disclosure.

'Why yes,' Mrs Ashton maintained, a frown puckering her neat features. 'A widowed lady, I collect, who made a great impression on my brother.'

'I am sure she did,' murmured Emily faintly, remembering her powerful personality. Surely her aunt was not proposing a match between that disparate pair! Emily was only now beginning to realize she had a matchmaking propensity; which was not the best quality in a chaperon.

Sophia, bored now the conversation had strayed from her favourite subject, quit the room.

'Do you think it wise,' asked Emily as soon as her sister had departed, 'to agitate Sophia with talk of marriage to this gentleman with whom she is clearly infatuated?'

'I forget how excitable the dear child is, you know,' admitted Mrs Ashton disarmingly. 'But I really do believe he will offer for her. I can say that now, since I know *you* are not setting your cap at him. They made such a delightful pair, I thought, when they sang together.'

As her aunt lapsed into the inevitable reminiscences about other duettists she had heard, Emily reflected that she was probably as wrong about Piers Aubery's intentions towards Sophia, as she was about her papa's opinion of the overwhelming Mrs Knowle.

Consequent upon this discussion with her aunt, Emily thought it only prudent to make it known to her father that should, by any remote possibility, an offer be received from Piers Aubery for her hand, she wished it to be rejected.

'But certainly, my dear,' Sir Ralph agreed readily. 'You know I would not have you marry against your will. But is there any particular reason for supposing the gentleman will make such an offer?'

'No, papa! Only Aunt Ashton's fancies upon the matter!'

'Ah yes — Mary,' he said as if that explained everything. 'But I thought these whimsies led her to believe it was Sophia who would receive the offer? Although how she reaches that addle-pated conclusion in a few weeks is beyond my comprehension!'

'And mine, I assure you. I do not believe there is the smallest foundation for any of it.'

'No, probably not . . . but I own I should not oppose a connexion with the Auberys, and nor, I collect, would Sophia!' he added, and Emily discerned a stray twinkle under the beetle-brows.

'I am persuaded she is suffering from a mere youthful infatuation, papa,' said Emily, taking the opportunity to influence her parent against what she was sure would be a disastrous match. Although why precisely she felt this she could not have explained.

'Perhaps . . . perhaps. But if I heed your wishes upon whom you should marry, it is only fair I should pay due regard to those of Sophia, is it not, my dear?'

So, on this incontestable but unsatisfactory note, the matter was left.

★   ★   ★

The day chosen by Ned Grimsby for their drive in Hyde Park was cold and wet, as the advent of May had brought no marked improvement in the weather. Consequently Ned merely paid the Marwoods a morning call and the expedition was postponed by mutual agreement until a future unspecified date.

Piers, however, anxious to keep pace with Ned's overtures to Miss Marwood, was unaware of this deferment when he asked his brother casually at the breakfast table one day:

'I wondered if I might borrow the barouche, Roly?'

Roland raised his brows. 'That sounds mighty staid for you, don't it? I thought you favoured the curricle.'

'In the ordinary way, yes, although I own I cannot particularly favour Judd's glum reproachful gaze upon my back constantly. I vow he wills me to overset the wretched thing so that he may complain to you! But with the barouche I can dispense with his services. Besides,' he added jauntily, 'the curricle won't accommodate two ladies.'

Harriet exchanged glances with Roly. 'You'll not tell us, I suppose, which two ladies?' she said.

'No, quite right, I won't!'

However neither twin had much doubt it was the Marwood sisters and permission was gladly granted. Since their introduction into Piers' life he had ceased to bombard Roland with odd schemes and outlandish characters demanding money: for that relief Roly was duly grateful, and he would be even more so if one of the young ladies could be prevailed upon to marry his brother and remove him from his sphere altogether.

Piers, who did not believe in deep-laid plans but preferred a gambler's approach to events, awaited the first moderately clear day and arrived that same morning at the Marwoods' door unheralded and with the barouche. He was lucky, and with his haphazard approach secured the Marwood sisters for a drive before the more meticulous Ned had succeeded in doing so. Insofar as furthering his acquaintance with the ladies was concerned, though, it was a hollow victory: Ned in his half-hour visit had talked chiefly with Emily and Sophia throughout the time; Piers in almost an hour's drive scarcely exchanged more than a few words with them, as he was on the forward box and they were seated behind him, with only the cut of his heavy many-caped coat to admire — for although it was fine it was not a warm day.

When he returned them to Great Stanhope Street — where one of the ubiquitous Marwood servants seemed to spring from nowhere to stand at the horses' heads whilst Piers handed the ladies down — both Emily and Sophia were full of praise for his driving skills.

'I vow I have never felt more secure in a carriage in my life,' declared Emily. 'You must be a nonpareil in the Four-in-Hand Club, I collect!'

'Unfortunately not, ma'am,' Piers admitted, not without a certain rancour as it had long been his ambition to join those exclusive ranks, but of course his pinchfist of a brother had not seen fit to supply the needful for the undertaking.

'Would you teach me to drive, sir?' asked Sophia. 'I would like it beyond all things, but our coachman is as old as Methuselah and such a slow-back.' Apart from which, Sir Ralph had expressly forbidden him to impart his driving skills to the daughters of the house.

If Emily entertained any misgivings about Piers' response they were short-lived.

'Nothing would please me more, ma'am, I do assure you, but I regret I must deny myself the pleasure. At the moment I have no suitable carriage at my disposal for the purpose.'

Before Sophia had the opportunity to put forward any suggestions on the matter — like asking papa to provide a vehicle — Emily intervened.

'Won't you step inside a moment, sir, for some refreshment?'

Had the invitation come only a few minutes before he would have seized upon it with enthusiasm, but the recent exchange about driving had quite put wooing heiresses from his impetuous mind. And so he declined, but with all his inherent charm and pleading a previous engagement of a most pressing nature, so that the young ladies were completely oblivious of the fact that, at that moment, all thought of them had been swept aside and replaced by yet another more riveting scheme for his advancement.

He had to see Roly right away . . .

5

Roland was at his desk trying to make a final decision about the mineral rights in Chelbeck Park. If Piers really was on the point of catching himself an heiress the drastic step of granting rights on their land might be avoided — for the moment, in any event. Head on hand, he ran a finger along his sturdy jaw-line. After a minute or two in this pensive attitude he drew the paper towards him and began to pen a letter to Henfield, the family lawyer, in rejection of the scheme.

He had barely completed the salutation when the door burst open and his young brother stood before him the very picture of glowing health and well-being: his cheeks, usually pale against the auburn curls, were whipped pink from the chilly drive and his eyes shone — whether from excitement or alarm was impossible to tell.

'Roly, I must speak to you!'

His voice lacked its customary polish and control: it must be alarm, thought Roland apprehensively. 'What's amiss? The barouche? Horses bolted?'

'Good God, no! What a monstrous suggestion!' he said with unwonted heat. 'Nothing's wrong! I've just made a decision affecting my whole future — and even *you* can't raise a dust over it this time!'

Roland leaned back in his chair and viewed his brother warily. Their dissimilarities were never more obvious than when Piers was expounding a new scheme and Roland was listening to it: agitation met calm; enthusiasm met caution; and finally, proposition met with rejection. But now Roland suddenly remembered his brother had been with the Marwood sisters that morning, and he grinned. 'By Jove, you don't let the grass grow under your heels, do you?'

'Never have — not if I'm given the

slightest encouragement.'

'I see,' said Roland, hastily revising his estimation of the modest Miss Marwood.

But Piers had ceased his restive pacing and fixed his brother with a suspicious eye. 'What do you mean? You can't know what my plans are — only known 'em myself for the past half hour!'

'It's pretty clear, if I may say so! You are patently a man whose proposal has just been accepted.'

'Hmph! Would that it had,' Piers said shortly, and in tones quite unlike a happy suitor's, but he soon brightened and added: 'But you will like it, Roly! Can't fail to.'

Roland's optimism began to fade. 'You are not contemplating entering the married state, then?'

'Married state! Who the devil said anything about marriage? Are you feeling quite the thing?' he asked with brief but genuine concern: it would be just like Roly to have a loose screw when he had finally evolved the perfect proposition for him.

'Yes, I am, thank you,' Roland said tersely, 'but I daresay you will put a period to that in the next few minutes . . . I take it you have a fresh plan? Well, you'd best tell me, I suppose.'

'Dammit, that's what I've been trying to do this past five minutes, but you were maundering on about marriage! Lord knows why!'

'Never mind! Your scheme?' Roland said, more gloomily than usual on these occasions, as only a moment ago he had been contemplating a rosy future when Piers' projects would be supported by Marwood money and not his own.

'In vulgar parlance — rattlers! It is the stage-coach for me from this day hence!' announced Piers with some drama. 'No call to look toplofical, Roly! Without undue conceit I think I may lay claim to possessing every quality needed for the venture — a skill with a team which can't be out-matched by any of your Corinthian cronies at the Four-in-Hand Club,' he said, unable to resist this envious gibe at his brother even at such a critical point, 'an eye for a prime bit of blood, an ability which is unsurpassed to — '

'You may spare me your declamations,' protested Roland, with some amusement, 'I am no coachmaster.'

'This, Roly, is the supreme moment, the golden opportunity for coaching! The roads are constantly improving, as is the comfort of the stages themselves — or so I believe,' he added with a rare flash of candour, for he had never travelled by stage in his life. 'Mine will equal the mails in expedition — ten miles in the hour I shall guarantee my customers!'

'Nor am I a customer!' Roland objected again. 'Piers,' he added quickly, 'I do not look down my nose at the idea, I assure you. I think it one of your best.'

Piers ceased his perambulation about the cramped room, seized a chair and straddled it. 'You do?' he asked earnestly.

'Certainly — although it will be arduous, have you considered that? Oh, I know you are no weakling, but a full-laden coach and maybe six-in-hand will need more than dexterous handling.' There was also all-night travelling and harsh weather to be faced, not to mention the fact that it would scarcely make a rich man of him, however bountiful the tips he received, but if he really wanted to drive a stage-coach he was not going to discourage him. 'Ned was saying only the other day that some of his fellow officers were to be found on the box these days — so you will not be in bad company. Why, even Worcester is one of their number, I collect.'

'Indeed yes, only the best will do for Piers Aubery!'

It was here that a maggot of doubt entered Roland's mind. 'Whom do you intend to approach upon the matter?' he asked tentatively.

'Why you, Roly! As if I would offer a chance like this to anyone else!'

'I had gained the impression you were going to offer your services as a stage driver to one of the proprietors,' Roland observed in a bleak voice.

'Never said so! Do you suppose I have no pride? As if I would sink so low! No — I shall put my own coach on the road, one especially built for speed. The Chelbeck Charger I thought I would call her. Doesn't that have a splendid ring to it?' he asked rhetorically. 'And I shall have my own teams of horses, of course — oh, nothing ambitious at first,' he went on hastily, noting his brother's expression assume its customary discouraging aspect. 'London to Brighton, perhaps, or Newmarket. No, I have it! Dover! — Yes, Dover. To carry all the continental travellers.'

'Who seem to be mostly bankrupts escaping to Calais at the moment,' murmured Roland sardonically, thinking of Brummell and others like him.

'You expect me to invest in this venture? Have you any idea what it will cost?'

'No, none,' he replied cheerfully, 'but I can soon find out. I thought of toddling over to Liquorpond Street later to have a word with Collingridge.'

'Dammit, Piers, there's no need to have the Regent's coachbuilder to rummage up a stage, is there?'

'*Rummage up* a stage! — you don't seem to grasp the implications of my idea . . . '

'On the contrary, I do! Only too well! Look,' Roland said in earnest tones, 'I have no wish to trample on every idea you have, and I do believe this could work out capitally — but only if you are prepared to apply yourself to its creation wholeheartedly — '

'Oh, I am,' his brother assured him.

'Well . . . if you mean that and will be singleminded and practical about the whole affair,' (even as Roland said this he thought how unlikely it sounded, but he was determined to give Piers one last chance), 'and if you will endeavour to keep the expenditure to the minimum — and that means no royal coachbuilders! — I will consider it. Let me have a rough estimate of what the venture might cost initially. I would suggest you try to buy a carriage at the Long Acre warehouse,' he proposed deflatingly, then compounded the effect by adding in business-like tones: 'How much can you contribute from your allowance?'

'Allowance?' Piers shifted uneasily. 'What would I live on?'

'Not above half the year has passed and it is more than enough to live on, you know. You could support a comfortable establishment on less.' Roland had fixed the sum initially at a high level in the hope his brother would strike out and set up an independent household, but he had preferred to squander all his income on his own pleasures and appearance, and to share the Aubery house and servants.

Piers passed his affairs under quick mental review and concluded he had barely two hundred pounds left, together with a number of resty creditors. He had hoped for an outright payment from Roly to launch the Chelbeck Charger, from which he could also pay off some of his more pressing duns . . . Still, he was always of a philosophical tendency where his, and particularly other people's money was concerned. 'I daresay I can manage a monkey towards it,' he offered airily, with not the least notion where the other three hundred pounds would come from, or what he would live on meanwhile — other than the long-suffering creditors. However, it was only diplomatic to humour Roly at this stage of the proceedings.

'Five hundred,' repeated Roland thoughtfully and turned the matter over in his mind: if Piers would commit half of his allowance it might concentrate his interest on the scheme for longer than was usual with his ideas: also, this was the first time Roland had felt inclined to lend any support to his brother as he did consider this to be a trifle less buffle-headed than his earlier notions. He had no real belief that it would keep Piers wholly out of mischief — for nothing could — but if he took it at all seriously it would occupy most of his time. 'Yes, Piers, I like your scheme and am willing to frank it . . .'

But he had no time to voice any of his reservations and conditions before Piers had disentangled himself from the chair and was leaning across the desk to grasp his brother's hand. 'You're a great gun, Roly! Always said so! You won't regret it, I promise you that!'

'No, indeed I shan't if I can help it,' he said with a wry smile, regaining possession of his hand, 'for I intend to keep a close eye on my investment. Look into the matter as thoroughly as maybe and let me know the costs involved . . . for the coach, for the minimum number of cattle — you'd best ride the route you intend to fix upon, have a word with the landlords at suitable inns for their charges — '

'All right, all right,' said Piers tetchily, 'the Chelbeck Charger is *mine*, you know.'

'Not yet it isn't!' Roland grinned at him. 'Oh, don't fret, I shan't throw a blight over the project as long as you are prepared to take the matter seriously.'

'You see before you Piers Aubery, coachmaster, about to set forth to Liquorpond — '

'Long Acre,' interjected Roland.

'Ah yes, Long Acre, to be sure,' amended Piers smoothly.

'And no transaction to be entered into until I have seen some extent of the expenditure needed, remember,' Roland cautioned his incorrigible brother.

'Oh, certainly not!' Piers shook his head in an appalled fashion at the very idea, as he took his leave.

A faint smile played about Roland's lips for a while as he stared at the recently closed door then he, too, shook his head . . .

A moment later he found himself looking down at the letter he had been about to write to Henfield rejecting the idea of selling mineral rights. He tore this up now without hesitation: for who could say when he might need more funds to keep the Chelbeck Charger on the road?

Piers was not home for dinner but there was nothing unusual in this and Harriet did not remark upon the fact.

'I have not returned an answer yet to the Marwoods' invitation. I must do so tomorrow,' Harriet said to her twin, who had been silent hitherto — but then this was another perfectly usual circumstance between them. 'Shall you attend? I need not consult Piers on the matter, I know! I shall take his acceptance for granted.'

'Then you may be wrong,' Roland informed her. 'You forget how mercurial our young brother is.'

'I do not! But as he was only this morning driving them around the park I thought it reasonable to suppose . . . '

She looked across at her twin. 'Was it not the Marwood sisters, after all?'

'Do you know I don't believe he said — but it scarcely signifies who it was! Piers has another scheme on hand, you see.'

'Oh no! How is he proposing to contrive your ruin this time?'

Roland told her. ' . . . but I'm not altogether unhopeful of the idea. He does possess a number of talents which, if they aren't misapplied, would certainly make a success of an undertaking of this sort. In any event, I decided to give him the benefit of the doubt — just once more.'

'I think that was very generous of you, Roly.'

'Yes, well, we won't delve into the reasons for that,' he responded briskly, not wanting a discussion about Piers' doubtful parentage again. 'Some might take a more uncharitable view and say I was out of my wits.'

'I do so hope he makes a success of it. I am persuaded he has only lacked an absorbing occupation, you know,' Harriet said in bracing tones, whether to reassure Roland or herself it was hard to tell.

Her twin did not feel inclined to comment upon this observation, and after a pause Harriet remarked casually: 'I was quite convinced he was casting out lures to Miss Marwood . . . This is not a preliminary to setting up in the married state, is it?'

'Lord, no! He looked utterly blank when I mentioned matrimony to him today.'

'Oh . . . Well then, shall we attend the Marwoods' dance, Roly? It may look a trifle odd if we all decline. Ned is going, I collect,' she added in a careless fashion.

But it did not deceive Roland. 'Then I suggest we go and keep an eye on him,' he said wickedly.

'I don't know what you mean!' Harriet exclaimed, a flush of indignation making her look like a young girl, in spite of the matronly cap she wore.

'I believe you do!' Roland said, then appeared to leave the subject. 'I own I cannot be altogether sorry if Piers does not wed Miss Marwood after all. She impresses me as a young lady of great sensibility and understanding whose qualities would be quite thrown away as Piers' wife.'

'I agree with you absolutely; I have found her to be everything you say — and surely those very attributes would make it inevitable she would reject Piers' suit?'

'You are disregarding the unscrupulous charm which he can exercise over any female! — *and* you are forgetting the father. Sir Ralph is a great stickler for the old conventions, I would hazard, and if he gave the match his blessing I cannot see Miss Marwood defying him.'

'I would not be too certain upon that head — she does not lack spirit. However, it is a situation which seems unlikely to arise now,' she said, not without a hint of regret, Roland thought.

'Well, that leaves the field open for Ned, does it not?' her twin proposed brutally. 'You must have noticed his particular interest in her. Now that would be a more acceptable match all round, I fancy.'

Harriet stared fixedly at her plate. 'Yes, I suppose so,' she agreed in a colourless tone.

'Can't understand why he hasn't come up to scratch and renewed his offer to you since he came home,' Roland went on with apparent heedlessness, although he was not enjoying his self-imposed and unnatural role of blundering brother. 'I always thought the two of you would eventually — '

Goaded beyond endurance at last, she cried: 'Stop it, Roly!' She bit her lip, then said in a detached manner: 'He did ask me to marry him almost as soon as he returned from the continent.'

Roland waited for her to continue and watched her averted face closely, but she remained silent. 'Then

116

why —?' he began eventually.

'Oh, a dozen reasons!' she burst out. 'The chief of which was that I thought he was renewing his offer primarily because of a sense of obligation . . . He knew it was expected of him when he sold out — expected by his family, by you, and by me, of course!'

'So — what answer did you return?' Roland asked, his voice resuming its customary gentleness.

'No!' she said, with a tight smile.

'Very chilling.'

'Yes — he offered to cut the connexion between our families, of course, but I said that was not necessary — or fair to you, his good friend — and that I was prepared to be sensible and maintain our relationship as it was.'

'Even more chilling,' murmured Roland to himself. 'Well,' he went on briskly, 'I must own you have achieved that in the most convincing manner, and if it threw the dust in my eyes it would surely fool anyone — for I had no notion when this catastrophe occurred!'

'Catastrophe!' she echoed. 'That is pitching it a bit strong, isn't it?'

'Is it?' His grey eyes sought out her identical ones, but she pushed back her chair suddenly.

'If you will excuse me,' she murmured. 'Oh — what *shall* I do about the Marwood invitation? Refuse for us all?'

'I would advise you accept for all,' Roland said drily. 'We can always make Piers' excuses for him — and who knows what he might be doing a fortnight hence?'

6

Sir Ralph, who had never been known to express interest in such matters before, insisted upon Mrs Knowle being invited to the forthcoming entertainment at Great Stanhope Street — which had developed from a modest dance for the young people into a somewhat heterogeneous gathering of old and young.

At their first meeting Mrs Knowle had expressed a passion for whist — which was evidently unrequited under her nephew, Lord Bittadon's, roof — and Sir Ralph had confessed to her his own weakness for the game. 'Regrettably, though,' he told her, 'I have abandoned the pursuit these past years because of failing sight. My late wife, bless her, always partnered me, and had the patience of a saint with my slowness with the cards, but I would not inflict myself on anyone now.'

'I've never heard such humbug!' Mrs Knowle had declared in her outspoken way. 'If it is a whist partner you want you need look no further — I lay no claims to being a saint, mind!' She had given one of her hearty laughs at this point, which in itself might have been expected to repel the decorous Sir Ralph. But this was far from being the case as a startled Emily was to realise when Mrs Knowles attended their party — which had now diversified into a card-party, musical entertainment, supper and, almost incidentally, a dance for the youthful company.

There had been not a single refusal from the invitations despatched, and Emily could not help reflecting with some satisfaction what a salutary effect their chance meeting with the Auberys had had upon their social life. Word had travelled fast among their old, and largely Kentish acquaintance that Lord Bittadon and his family would be present, and this had created a new surge of interest in the hitherto unexciting gatherings at Great Stanhope Street. Emily, however, was simply pleased that, with Mrs Grimsby and Ned — and not forgetting the redoubtable Mrs Knowle — six agreeable people had been added to their circle of acquaintance.

Early in the evening Aunt Ashton had fixed upon Mrs Grimsby, and as both ladies were of an anecdotal turn they had detached themselves from the company and settled in a quiet corner; it would have taken an intrepid soul to interrupt them, thought Emily, and none did. Consequently Emily was fully occupied as hostess and chaperon and as, in addition to this, her attention was frequently diverted by the spectacle of her father dealing amazingly well with the blatant Mrs Knowle, she was scarcely aware that Ned Grimsby was at her side rather more frequently than the other gentlemen. In his obtrusive way he was of great assistance, though, and she was grateful to him for discerning that she lacked support from her own family. Sophia, of course, was taking the opportunity to flirt with not only Mr Aubery but all the eligible gentlemen present: her own surroundings seemed to have lent her still greater confidence.

If Emily attached no significance to Ned's help at the time beyond thinking gratefully that his was a thoughtful and complaisant nature, Piers saw in it a sharp reminder of the threat to his erstwhile ambition to wed Miss Marwood. The period of his burning interest in the stage-coach venture had passed now: all was prospering and the Chelbeck Charger would soon be taking to the road. This had not been achieved without some temporary difficulties, and a vastly higher investment in the project than Roly would have been prepared to stump up — but a figure adjusted here and there on the tradesmen's estimates for his brother's perusal had met the case, and everyone was happy.

Even Piers, however, foresaw an

eventual reckoning, and his flexible mind had at once returned to thoughts of heiresses. Acting as always on the precept that he who hesitates is lost, the moment he saw Ned answer a summons from his mother, he went immediately to Emily's side.

'My dear Miss Marwood, you will be quite exhausted by your onerous duties as hostess! I would be honoured to be permitted to fetch your supper to you — but only if you promise to sit quietly with me for a time, otherwise I fear you will be too fatigued to dance later. That would mean the company was deprived of its best dancer — which is not to be thought of.'

The brilliant blue eyes, which had enchanted him at their first meeting, sparkled in appreciation. 'I cannot believe such fine words from one whom I consider to be by far the most skilful exponent of the art I have seen.'

'I swear I would not offer you Spanish coin, ma'am, I have far too great a regard for you for that.' The look which accompanied this declaration surprised Emily by its intensity. 'So — if we are both correct in our estimations, ergo we are the best couple on the floor, and that is all the more reason for you to be fresh for the dancing! I give you warning now — I shall insist upon two dances at the very least! Now, you must tell me what to bring you from the sumptuous array of dishes in the other room, and then I shall return and explain why I shall be forever indebted to you!'

He departed on this intriguing note and she reflected that it was not difficult to see why Sophia should entertain such an ungovernable passion for him: he did not lack charm, and when it was accompanied by evident sincerity it was almost irresistible. But Emily could never quite eliminate the qualifying 'almost'. The thought of her young sister made her look anxiously about her: she finally caught a glimpse of Sophia regarding an earnest and voluble admirer — whom Emily recognised as one of their Hollsted acquaintance — with a look of acute boredom, so for the moment she was out of mischief . . .

Piers returned with a footman and two laden plates, and guided Emily to an unoccupied window-seat. 'No monstrous crush, a surfeit of seating, and as many attendants as one could wish for! No, I fear you can never hope to aspire to the ranks of the *à la mode* hostesses, ma'am, if you maintain these standards,' Piers observed ironically.

'Then I shall be well-satisfied, I assure you,' Emily responded with a smile.

'As indeed you should be! Now let me explain why I owe you such a debt of gratitude. If you will cast your mind back to our drive — and how wretched has been the weather ever since!' he interpolated, suggesting that had it been otherwise there would have been subsequent outings. 'You may remember you were kind enough to say a word in praise of my driving skill. I am persuaded you were merely being polite, but nonetheless that generous remark set me thinking, and the outcome of those thoughts has quite revolutionized my life!'

'You alarm me, sir!' Emily declared, but with a humorous glint in her eye. 'I have not the smallest wish to foster revolutions — papa would disown me for much less!'

Even in jest, the mere thought of such a consequence sent a tremor through her listener. 'It was an unfortunate choice of phrase, forgive me! I shall say instead it has wrought a transformation — for, where I had no occupation I now have a life's interest. In short, I am set fair to becoming the most notable coachmaster in the county! I have told no one outside the family as yet and I wanted you to be the first to know.' This contained a grain of truth, for although Piers' latest crack-brained venture was the talk of the clubs, he had not actually mentioned it to an acquaintance before.

Emily could not have been more surprised had he said he was setting up as brewer, or haberdasher, or anything else for that matter: she had never associated him with an occupation of any description. It seemed she had misjudged him in regarding him as a mere dilettante and fashionable gentleman . . .

Piers had not meant to divulge his intentions to the Marwoods in case it should damage his chances of obtaining Sir Ralph's blessing to a match with one of his daughters, but he had suddenly had the desire to share his news with Miss Marwood. 'I have shocked you, I can see! You regard it as trade, I daresay . . . '

'Oh no! Pray do not misunderstand — I am somewhat overawed by the weight of responsibility, that is all! To be credited with fashioning someone's future is no light matter, you must see that!' And this time she did not believe him: no one would base such a momentous decision on a casual remark — so why had he interpreted it so?

'Oh, I do, and I have said how grateful I am for it! But I believe my fortunes changed for the better from the moment we met at Somerset House.'

'That must surely be a coincidence,' she said prosaically, feeling a trifle uneasy at the direction the conversation was taking. 'But I am glad, of course, whatever the root of it and I wish you every success with your venture. Tell me about it, for I must confess it sounds so much more interesting than going into the church or the law!' She thought he looked the part, too, with those curling sidewhiskers, just like a coachman's.

'I thought so, certainly! Miss Marwood,' he went on, with an ominous note of solemnity creeping into his voice, and this, coupled with the fact he had set aside his plate — not the most romantic of adjuncts — alerted Emily for a declaration of some sort. She looked about her and luckily caught the attention of one of their ubiquitous footmen. ' — there is another matter concerning my future,' he continued in the same earnest tone.

'Do forgive me,' she interrupted as the servant approached. 'I must defer hearing about your plans until later, I fear. I have my reputation to maintain as an unfashionable hostess, have I not?' she said lightly, and rose to consult the footman about making ready for the dancing . . .

Much to his chagrin Piers found himself partnering the young school-room sister, as he regarded her, for the first dance: for Ned, with his customary careful provision, had made sure of leading the dancing with Emily. However, before the night was out, they each had two dances with their hostess so honours were even there, thought Piers with satisfaction, and he must be running a neck ahead of Ned in the matrimonial stakes for certain, after his agreeable talk with the lady — even though it had been curtailed at the crucial moment.

Emily had carried off the interruption so smoothly that he had been quite unaware she had contrived it and, in any event, he decided subsequently that it was all for the best: the moment was not propitious for a marriage offer, and a glimpse of Sir Ralph, clearly an exacting and old-fashioned parent, convinced him it would be more conformable to approach him upon the matter first. However, to his surprise, he realised that night that he spoke no less than the truth when he said he had a genuine regard for Miss Marwood — indeed his feelings were much stronger even than that.

Nonetheless, it could not be said that his approach to Roly on the subject of marriage the next day was prompted wholly by his attachment to Miss Marwood; although his brother, had he been apprised of the fact, would have been astonished by its existence at all.

The brothers had been drawn together in the past week or so rather more than was usual over the creation of the stage-coach undertaking, so Piers was able to approach Roly in an informal manner.

They had been studying a map of Kent, and Piers had pointed out the details of his recently completed itinerary to Dover and back. As Piers rolled up the map his brother said:

'I must own you have been as painstaking as need be over this whole business. I am really very impressed.'

'Thank you, my lord,' Piers replied, with a stiff inclination of the head.

'Now, don't take huff! I didn't intend to sound patronising — I mean it! I do believe you have found your *métier* at last, and there seems to be no doubt you have selected the best route to ensure your establishment. If you can offer a service as speedy as posting for those wanting to catch the Dover packet — and much cheaper — it seems you will meet with little competition.'

'Yes,' agreed Piers, relenting, 'I

confess I had no idea how admirable the Dover Road was for the scheme when I proposed it.' It was true there wasn't much rivalry from other stage-coaches and this was largely because they could not offer a service to match the post-chaises: but then it was unlikely Piers could do so either at a reasonable cost. He had uncovered some disquieting facts — the prime one being that a horse a mile was reckoned to be the requirement for fast coaches, and that meant he should have seventy cattle available on the Dover Road. Roland, of course, was basing his enthusiasm upon doctored accounts, and he had no intention of disillusioning him at this delicate stage in the operation. 'I shan't carry fish, in any event,' he said banteringly, 'and that should be an incentive to the discerning traveller!'

'When will you hope to be ready to take to the road? I can't wait to see the Chelbeck Charger in all its glory — what are its colours?'

'Purple and gold body with scarlet wheels — and bearing our crest, of course. It must be set apart from the carriages of lesser distinction! As to its launching — I would hope the end of next month would see all ready for the road.'

'Capital! I shan't be returning into Northamptonshire until early July. You know I almost envy you! All I have to look forward to is a poor hay harvest and a worse one for the wheat — and the lugubrious Beechers to tell me with relish every disastrous detail of it all!'

In his new role of responsible gentleman of affairs Piers looked suitably grave and asked: 'Are we really going to be under the hatches, Roly?'

Heartened by the genuine note of concern in his young brother's voice he responded bracingly: 'Oh, I daresay we shall come about! The Auberys have had bad harvests before now and survived, and if we have a brilliant summer eventually, it may not be all Stygian gloom. However, should the worst happen there are still the Chelbeck mineral rights, loth though I am to grant them.'

'I see . . . I was asking partly in regard to my situation if I should decide to marry sometime.' He said it in as detached a manner as possible but Roland still looked up sharply. 'The arrangement was, I fancy,' Piers continued, 'that I should have four thousand pounds in that event.'

'Why yes, and you must know I would not dream of putting that in jeopardy.' They were both aware that it had been at his mother's request that such a sum should be set aside to be paid to Piers on the occasion of his marriage. She had intended it as a small recompense for his invidious position in the family, although at the time she had not been able to foresee he would apply himself to the matter of obtaining requital with the utmost diligence, long before he attained the married state. 'And there is the Grange at Chelbeck, of course, which in the common run would bring you a comfortable income, as well as providing a most attractively snug home for your bride.' Roland forebore to mention that if Piers had not indulged in so many meaningless acts of generosity with the Aubery fortune, he would have gladly augmented the four thousand pounds himself.

'Less than ever do I see myself as a country gentleman lording in at the Grange, with my own particular Beechers to contend with — no, I shall hold to my resolve to be a coaching proprietor of the first stare!' It had not escaped Piers' notice that Hollsted Manor, the Marwoods' country seat, lay just off the Dover Road, a circumstance he regarded as fortuitous in the extreme — for what more natural than that Miss Marwood should wish to remain within easy distance of her ageing parent when she married? There was bound to be a suitable dwelling for the purpose on the Hollsted estate, which his preliminary enquiries had discovered to be extensive. All in all, the auguries were excellent for the match and he was increasingly convinced that it was meant to be; however, all he said now was: 'I felt I had to take a muster of the position. After all, I have squandered above four thousand in the past year or two — I know it! And if you had been a veritable nipfarthing you might have recouped your losses from that sum, and who could blame you for it!'

Roland was momentarily struck dumb by this burst of self-knowledge and, as he was meant to, was completely diverted from asking Piers if he had any immediate intention of getting leg-shackled. At last he found his voice. 'But bear in mind if you don't keep the line in this new venture I may turn pinchfist yet, so beware!'

Piers could not be sure, in spite of the accompanying laugh, that there was not a seed of truth in what Roly said. There was no time to be lost, that much was clear: he was not keeping the line, as Roly put it, with the Chelbeck Charger, and sooner or later that would be discovered.

By the time he left his brother, he had decided to see Sir Ralph without delay to ask for the hand of his elder daughter in marriage.

★　★　★

Emily was grateful to Mr Aubery for one circumstance: since Sophia had developed her overwhelming affection for him she had gradually become less of a hurly-burly female and was much given instead to long periods of rapturous day-dreaming.

'How long do you suppose that poor child will wear the willow for Mr Aubery?' Mrs Ashton speculated two days after their highly successful dance.

'You make it sound as though someone had died, aunt! Besides, Sophia was quite as flirtatious as I would wish her to be, the other evening. If she were fancy free her behaviour would be beyond the line of what is pleasing — of that I am tolerably certain.'

'Well, there may not be many weeks left now before we return into Kent,' Mrs Ashton announced, determined to cast a gloom. 'Sir Ralph is anxious to be home as soon as maybe because of this dreadful weather . . . Really, I can scarcely see to set a stitch this morning! I do believe there must be a storm threatening. I have not known a spring like this one since — '

'Yes, it is bad. I will ring for some working candles,' Emily offered, and went across to the bell-pull.

'Oh no! I did not mean — oh, think of the expense!' protested Mrs Ashton, who could never grow accustomed to the lavishness of the Marwood establishments.

'I will not let you strain your eyes for the want of a wax candle . . . Yes, I know papa would return to Hollsted tomorrow if he could, but I have done my utmost to convince him he would

138

not improve the weather one jot by doing so! At least in town we can enjoy a few diversions however much rain falls, but I fancy the country lanes must be quite impassable with mud.' Emily looked out of the window at the eerie lowering sky, whilst she waited for the candles to be brought. 'But to return to Sophia — I would be glad, of course, if she could meet a suitable parti this season, but I scarcely regard it as a tragedy if she does not. After all, she is not out yet and the few social gatherings she is attending will serve to give her a bit of town bronze for next year.'

'You are quite right, of course,' agreed the pliable Mrs Ashton. 'It is greatly to be hoped that you were correct in your surmise that Mr Aubery was on the point of declaring himself to you, for that would be the most desirable outcome imaginable.'

Emily turned from the window and viewed her relative with some exasperation. 'But, aunt, I have said consistently

I would not accept him, and indeed I mentioned my suspicions to you only so that you should refrain from encouraging Sophia in her girlish transports. I own I may be mistaken about his intentions towards me, but nonetheless I cannot believe he has shown the least attachment to Sophia.'

'Oh dear, that may be so I suppose, but I did think I intecepted a *particular* look between them during the cotillion — and that was the *first* dance of the evening, was it not?'

Emily found she could not stay out of humour with the feather-brained Aunt Ashton for very long. She smiled and said: 'You are an incurable romantic — ' A noise outside the window took her attention. 'Hallo, we have a caller. Now who is intrepid enough to brave the coming storm, I wonder?' She thought it was Ned, but when the gentleman raised his beaver-hatted head and squared his shoulders before approaching the door she knew it wasn't he.

The disappointment she experienced at this realization surprised her a little. Certainly she liked Ned and found his company most enjoyable but her feelings towards him went no deeper than this for the moment. However, Mrs Grimsby had evidently opened her heart to Aunt Ashton during their long confabulation, and had revealed that her son was a rejected suitor of Harriet. When Emily recalled the seemingly easy relationship between the couple she thought how well-suited they appeared to be, and wondered what had gone wrong. It was difficult to discover from Aunt Ashton's confused reportage exactly how matters stood between them now — if indeed anyone knew — but Mrs Grimsby was trying to propel her son into matrimony, it seemed, by hinting that she would leave the ancestral home and move into a dower-house on their estate.

Emily did not feel she deceived herself in thinking that Ned had shown a particular interest in her since they had met, and she inevitably wondered how she would respond should he propose. She was beginning to suspect her answer might be in the affirmative ...Well, he hadn't called this morning, but she had no doubt that the gentleman outside would interest her aunt no less than Ned Grimsby.

Mrs Ashton had just received her expensive working candles but had no compunction about leaving them to join her niece at the window. 'Oh, my dear, it is Mr Aubery himself! What a shame Sophia is gone to the Rogers for her singing lesson!' exclaimed that incorrigible lady.

'Well, he hasn't called with the intention of taking us for a drive in the park this time!' Emily said drily, eyeing the dashing two seat curricle.

'I do so hope he does not get caught in the coming downpour. A thorough soaking can so easily fly to the chest and cause the onset of a consumptive tendency. Your two cousins have the most distressing disregard for such consequences, I may say. I remember one dreadful day when they rode to see the . . . '

Whilst Aunt Ashton reminisced about her two lusty sailor sons Emily wondered if they contrived to keep bone dry at sea — a hazard which fortunately did not seem to have occurred to their doting mama. However, as George's ship was due in to Portsmouth in the next few weeks, and Henry was making his first voyage as lieutenant, Emily had no difficulty in diverting her aunt's mind from Mr Aubery's visit, when it became clear he was not going to be shown in to see them. She enquired about her cousins' latest letters — although it could not be said she succeeded in banishing their visitor from her own thoughts. He must have come to see her father, and with his earnest manner still fresh in her mind she felt convinced he must have come to offer for her hand. If indeed he had, she hoped her papa would spare her any embarrassing interview with Mr Aubery.

Sophia returned from her lesson about a quarter of an hour after their visitor's arrival.

'Oh, I thought Mr Aubery was here,' she said; quite unnecessarily, as she had entered the room with remarkable dignity and an immaculate appearance. 'They are his things disposed in the hall, surely? I recognize his stylish hat anywhere.'

'Yes,' confirmed Emily, 'he is with papa, I believe.'

'What would he want to see him about?' Sophia asked.

'Perhaps he has changed his mind about selling his collection of paintings,' Emily responded with a flash of inspiration. She had not mentioned his coaching venture to anyone, but thought perhaps he might be in need of money to support it. Having thought of this plausible explanation, it calmed her a little.

'I do hope not!' exclaimed Sophia. 'For I'm sure it would break his heart!'

'I doubt that organ is quite as fragile as you suppose,' Emily said crushingly.

'How should you know? You don't love him as I do! He has such exquisite taste in all things . . . Did you notice his box coat that day he took us for a drive — six capes it had and gold buttons!'

'You had as well love his tailor, it seems!' Emily said teasingly, but young love had no humour and she knew no amount of ridicule would dissuade her sister from thinking that Piers Aubery was a paragon who embodied every virtue.

Twell came in to the room and said: 'The master wishes Miss Sophia to go up to the drawing-room, at once, if you please.'

'Me?' cried Sophia. 'Oh, what is it about, do you suppose? Is papa there, Twell?'

'I believe not, miss, but right away, he said.' He departed before the onset of more quizzing from his young mistress.

'It must be Mr Aubery who wants to see me! I know it is!' she said, working herself up into a fervour of excitement.

'Well, I know it isn't!' declared Emily. 'Papa would never countenance such a thing. Nor will he countenance being kept waiting — you had best go up to him.'

7

Unaware of two pairs of female eyes
fixed upon him from a nearby window,
Piers hesitated momentarily before
the Marwoods' door, squared his
shoulders, then mounted the few steps
in case he should change his mind.
He only experienced the briefest of
doubts, though, because Sir Ralph was
expecting him and it would look
very singular if he should miss such
a recently sought appointment, and
besides he entertained no real misgivings about his mission — just the
natural nerves of a young man about to
confront his future father-in-law.

His garb was the most unexception-
able sort he could devise for the
occasion, comprising brown superfine
tail-coat, buff pantaloons and tasselled
Hessians, and he had abandoned his
recently assumed style of neckcloth

— the Mail Coach — for a more restrained tie, designated the Oriental. However, although the results he had finally achieved with the snowy neck-cloth at the fourth attempt looked impressive, it was dashed uncomfortable and threatened to sever an ear-lobe with a hasty movement: in addition to this, the brown coat was one he had not worn for two years and was an unpleasant close fit. He silently cursed his brother for being too tight-fisted to employ a valet for himself, which meant Piers could not share his services. (In fact Roland's modest sartorial needs were attended to by his tiger, Judd, who had a variety of skills at his command. But this arrangement was condemned as ramshackle by Piers and he would have none of it.) He could have supported his own man out of his allowance, but what use that if he was then left with no funds to clothe himself decently?

The depressing realization that he must have put on rather more weight recently than he had imagined struck him just as he was shown into Sir Ralph's presence in the small book-room.

His host, however, took his careworn expression to be no more than a manifestation of the natural anxiety of a suitor: for he had assumed Mr Aubery's visit concerned one of his daughters. He had discovered that young men did not tend to call upon him these days for any other reason.

'Forgive me if I don't stir from my place. This damnable damp has crept into my joints and won't shift — and neither can I!'

The gruff tones of Sir Ralph emanated from the depths of a tall wing chair comfortably established by a blazing fire, and that, together with the leaden quality of the light filtering through the solitary window, made the scene more appropriate to December than late May.

Piers managed a courtly if somewhat restricted bow to his host.

149

'Sit down, sit down, sir,' instructed Sir Ralph a trifle edgily: he was not at his best that morning, and the prospect of steering a gentleman, who appeared quite rigid with apprehension, through the delicate complexities of marriage settlements and fine feelings, dismayed him. He would, as kindly as possible, abridge the interview: after all, he knew the young man's case was hopeless if it was Emily's hand he sought, and the sooner he was apprised of that the better.

'I'd rather stand if you don't mind, sir,' Piers said, nervously inserting a slim hand in the strained buttons of his coat in a Napoleonic gesture.

'As you will . . . Well, now, from the tenor of your letter, I collect, I am in the right of it in thinking you wish to approach me with a view to marrying one of my daughters?' Sir Ralph had started this speech staring into the flames but he fixed his hearer with one of his formidable looks at the conclusion.

Piers was taken aback by the directness and lack of finesse of this opening remark. After all, the situation was new to him, even if it was probably no novelty to Sir Ralph, and he had been rehearsing several possible gallant but circuitous introductory speeches, not omitting a smattering of reassuring hints as to his suitability and solid worth as a prospective son-in-law. In the event all he said was: 'Yes, sir, quite right.' And with his head held at a military angle by the constricting neckcloth, he felt as if he were on parade. It was not the sort of impression he had meant to give, but perhaps it was no bad thing, he thought philosophically: the less he said, the less chance there was of uttering a wrong word. He had a tendency to be a trifle effusive, perhaps, and Sir Ralph did not look to be the sort who could be flummeried.

In the poor light Sir Ralph could not see his visitor all that clearly and indeed, for a fleeting moment, he thought he looked devilish like young Grimsby with that military bearing. But it wouldn't do to confuse the two fellows at this juncture, by Jove! Emily would never forgive him!

'First of all,' explained Sir Ralph, 'I do not wish you to labour under a misapprehension that I am the kind of parent who orders his daughters as if they were so many chattels. I have a very good understanding of their wishes in these matters — perhaps I have made a particular push to do this because of their unfortunate lack of a mother's care — and have thus saved one or two gentlemen the embarrassment of a personal rebuff from the lady of his choice. So, before we proceed further in this affair — have you ascertained whether the young lady herself is agreeable to your proposal?'

'No, sir.' Again, Piers would have expanded upon this, but the interview had proceeded so differently from his expectation that he was quite unnerved: besides, he thought with sinking spirits, it didn't sound too promising.

'Well, I hope I do not appear brutal but I must be cruel only to be kind, if you understand me. If your choice has alighted upon my elder daughter, Emily, I fear I must disappoint you. You will realise I can say no more upon the matter than that, but you may rest assured I would not speak without absolute authority.'

Luckily Sir Ralph's gaze had drifted back to the firelight during this speech so he did not witness the brief dismay on his hearer's face: had it not been a physical impossibility, because of the encroaching presence of the Oriental, Piers' jaw would have dropped. But at once his volatile brain realised he had some very rapid thinking to do. It seemed that Ned had outstripped him for Miss Marwood's hand, but was it then safe to assume that the young sister — the schoolroom miss — was likely to be willing? (God, what was her name?) And if she was, did he want to marry her? No, that wasn't the question at all — would it solve his problems if he did marry her? Well, for all he knew the sisters might have been given equal portions, and he would incur no financial loss from the change . . . Oh, Lord, the old boy had stopped talking!

'No, I do not think it brutal in the smallest degree, sir, that you should be so frank and open upon this very vital matter,' improvised Piers wildly. Should he or shouldn't he offer for Susan — Sarah — no, what the devil was it? She had a pretty voice, he remembered irrelevantly. *Sophia!* That was it! The sheer relief at having recalled her name in time tipped the balance: he *would* offer for her! 'Of course,' he went on, with a shade more calm, 'had Miss Marwood been the object of my affections I might have felt somewhat differently, I daresay!' He even managed a laugh at this point, which sounded a trifle strangled to his ears for reasons other than the cursed neckcloth. But fortunately for him he was in a situation which could excuse an overwrought state, and Sir Ralph considered it nothing untoward.

'Ah, so it is my little Sophia, is it?' he said, supplying the elusive name to Piers should he have needed it still. Sir Ralph had felt a slight pang of disappointment upon hearing this, but not for any more overpowering reason than that he was in the greatest discomfort with his rheumatics and had hoped to curtail the interview at that point. Although he adjudged Piers to be a sound Tory and of an agreeable disposition, he was pleased that Emily was not to wed him: for whoever married her would eventually inherit the Hollsted estate, and whatever Mr Aubery was, he was not a country gentleman born and bred. 'Well, you must approach her yourself, of course, but I hazard you will not meet with a rejection there. However, much depends upon the favourable outcome of our discussion now, as I am sure you will understand,' he went on in business-like tones, causing his hearer's fluctuating spirits to suffer another relapse.

'Indeed, sir, and depend upon it although I do not believe the regard and depth of affection I have for your daughter could be called into question, I am fully aware of my inadequacies in other respects. A second son can never have as much to offer a wife as he would wish.' He paused a moment. 'My elder brother, however, does seem disinclined for marriage, and there remains therefore some possibility I might inherit one day,' he continued, pusillanimously deferring particular discussion of his current financial position: there was, he was tolerably certain, no move afoot in the family to disinherit him because of his irregular parentage — it was, after all, a situation far from unique.

'I tell you frankly, Mr Aubery, I set no great store by titles — there is good and bad blood in the peerage as anywhere else — but lineage is a different matter, and I happen to know that the late Lord Bittadon, and his father before him were excellent men both — so we'll say no more on that head.'

Piers sighed with considerable relief: no club tittle-tattle could have reached Sir Ralph's ears for many a long year.

'So!' continued Sir Ralph with more sharpness than he intended, having just sustained a particularly piercing twinge in his leg. 'What do you bring to my daughter other than affection, sir?'

All recollection of the bland speech he had prepared on the subject faded under that gelid stare and he stammered out his assets and income baldly. My God, he thought, it's hopeless: this downy old cove will never part with a daughter to an obvious indigenous wastrel like me! An even more alarming thought followed hard upon this one — what if he *did* give his consent but did not bestow a substantial dowry upon his youngest daughter? There was no proof that the Marwoods' fortune had not dwindled like the Auberys' had of late. He had not intended to touch upon the matter of the Chelbeck Charger at this interview, thinking it would be wholly detrimental to his cause, but now, in desperation, he put it forward as a further asset. In truth, he was only just beginning to realise the enormity of this sudden change of prospective bride: he had a genuine fondness for Miss Marwood, and a belated stab of disappointment assailed him. No, he did not really care if his suit was rejected — there must be other heiresses, dammit! ' . . . Well, there it is, Sir Ralph. Bittadon is franking the venture,' he concluded as carelessly as his strangulating clothing would allow.

'Is he, indeed?' Sir Ralph was taken aback at this evidence of a practical streak in Mr Aubery; like Emily he had thought him a dilettante of the arts and no more. 'I own I have no great love for racketing dangerously about the countryside at ten miles to the hour, but I know you young people don't regard it.' He had no notion though, that Mr

Aubery would be driving the coaches himself — merely investing in a company. 'And if Bittadon thinks it a sound investment, who am I to argue with that?' he said, rapidly adding up the possible value of the Grange estate at Chelbeck, Mr Aubery's thousand pounds per annum, and the returns from the coaching company which, he was well prepared to believe, would multiply with the so-called 'progress' of transport: there was also, of course, Mr Aubery's collection of paintings, which he had modestly omitted to mention, and quite probably other assets of that nature, which would appreciate when the current depression of the market lifted. Yes, all in all, he was well-satisfied. Sophia would be over the moon at the prospect before her, and he was not unhappy to have her future settled: there was always a danger, when she was thrust upon the world next year, that she would fix upon some gazetted fortune hunter — and he was perfectly sure that Piers Aubery, scion of such an ancient Tory family, was not *that*. In addition, for all his lofty indifference on the subject, Sir Ralph could not but be mindful of the possible peerage and all that would go with it: for if Mr Aubery did not inherit, a son of his — and Sophia's — might.

'You have not dressed up your prospects in high-flown prose and I like that, Mr Aubery. I hope you won't take it ill if I say I thought you might have done so!' This flash of insight sent another tremor through his audience, who wished the old boy would put him out of his misery as soon as maybe. 'Now, to Sophia's expectations,' Sir Ralph said on cue, 'I have fixed that she shall receive thirty thousand pounds — which, I may say, is safely invested in Funds . . . '

Piers gave a gulp which, with the lethal hold the Oriental had on his throat, threatened to choke him to insensibility.

' . . . Although this sum will not become payable to her until she attains her twenty-fifth birthday: on her marriage she will have a dowry of a modest two thousand pounds — it would have been more but these are parlous times, as you know, Mr Aubery — but with her allowance of £500 a year, I am persuaded you can live very comfortably for the first years of your marriage.' Sir Ralph obligingly set out the sums for Piers, whilst that young man felt now that a noose was tightening about his neck.

' . . . that will be an income of fifteen hundred per annum (*only five hundred more than I have now*, thought Piers, *and a wife and establishment to support*) . . . six thousand pounds in capital (*the whole practically committed to the Chelbeck Charger already*) . . . and a comfortable little estate at Chelbeck for your residence (*which Piers had no intention of living in*) . . . I shall be sad, of course, to see my youngest daughter fixed so far away in Northamptonshire, for I do not travel abroad more than I need, nowadays

— but then, I daresay you will visit us often enough. To tell the truth, I suppose I had not anticipated losing her so soon — which was foolish of me!'

Piers seized upon this chance to order something to his liking. 'I did wonder, sir — ' He cleared his throat and started again, saying rather too loudly: 'I wonder if it might be agreeable to you, sir, for us to reside at Hollsted — at least for some part of the year? Perhaps there is a little cottage on your estate I could rent?' He was tolerably certain Sophia would not be expected to live in too mean a dwelling.

'Why, by all means! I know the very place. It has been allowed to run down abominably, and has been empty these two years, but I'm sure with some little attention it could be as snug a place as one would wish. I should be glad to see it taken in hand for it is a fine Elizabethan timbered house — not overlarge. It has twelve — or is it fifteen? — bedrooms, I forget, but there is a gallery there, which would house your paintings admirably. An expenditure of two or three thousand should see it habitable. There are forty acres of rough ground and woodland with it, I may say. Capital shooting! I take it you are partial to a bit of shooting, Mr Aubery?'

He wasn't: but at that moment if someone had done him the courtesy of handing him a gun he would have been well-prepared to aim it at himself. Instead, he took as deep a breath as he was able without bursting his coat buttons, restrained himself from clawing at his cravat in a desperate manner — for the heat in the little room seemed over-powering — and croaked: 'You are very kind, sir, I am deeply grateful.' For what, he wondered, reviewing the situation despairingly. A house which was going to take the best part of the marriage settlement to put to rights; a wife, a considerable staff, and — eventually — a nursery, to support — and all with only £500 a year more than he had at his disposal now! He had not forgotten the thirty thousand pounds — how could he? — but would he survive that long? And how many years was that, for pity's sake? Sophia looked a mere child . . .

'Ay, well, it don't do to rejoice too soon!' Sir Ralph said merrily, glad his part of the affair was concluded for the day. 'You've the young lady herself to face now.'

Before Piers could beg for a respite (stay of execution seemed the more apposite expression, he reflected) his host's gnarled hand had reached out for the bell-pull, and even now the butler would be on his way to escort him to the scaffold . . .

8

Before setting out from Bittadon House that morning, Piers had fortified himself with brandy and then, at Sir Ralph's behest, he had helped himself to another large neat glass of the spirit. Now, as he trod carefully the shallow stair to the drawing-room after Twell, the Marwood butler, he wished he had had time to take a glass of porter as a damper — although, on reflection, as he was proposing to the wrong lady for the wrong reasons it was perhaps as well to be a trifle bosky.

His sense of impending doom was heightened when he was left on his own in the large apartment and thunder rolled in the distance. My God, he thought, as a flash of lightning seemed to extinguish the small fire struggling in the grate, this is turning into a monstrous Gothic tragedy . . . or farce.

Yes, it was too ludicrous: how could he ask a young girl, whom he scarcely knew, to marry him for no reason except that he might possibly acquire her thirty thousand pounds six, seven or even eight years hence — by which time he would be nearly thirty years old himself and doubtless long resident in Calais with all the other bankrupt exiles ... Impetuous as ever, he was striding towards the door to effect his escape when he was struck by another unpleasant and more immediate thought — which was that if he left the Marwoods' house in such a hasty and unorthodox manner, he would be bound to sustain a thorough soaking in the deluge which must now be imminent. Roly, for certain, would have scoffed at this namby-pamby attitude in one proposing to drive a stage-coach in all weathers, but Piers checked only a few feet from the door, undecided and befuddled. There was a chance the lady might reject his offer, of course. Indeed, he could see no possible reason for her to accept him . . .

As to precisely what happened next he was never quite certain, except that the door opened, which seemed in turn to give rise to an immediate and nerve-shattering dazzle of lightning. Before he had time to focus his eyes properly on the agency which had precipitated this confusion, an overhead peal of thunder caused the new arrival to emit a small scream of terror. Realising it was Miss Sophia, scared out of her wits by the storm, he instinctively put his arm about her in a protective fashion. 'Easy, ma'am,' he said, as if to one of his panicky wheelers. He glanced up at the sudden tattoo at the windows. ' . . . Ah, here comes the rain — it will soon pass over now.'

His captive, torn between the bliss of this abrupt embrace and the feeling she should present herself as the sort of female who did not swoon in a mere thunderstorm, lingered as long as she dare and then drew away from him, saying with dignity (and truth), 'It was not the storm which alarmed me, sir, but your standing by the door! You see I was not at all certain whom I should find here,' she explained.

For a brief moment, as he held the plump Miss Sophia Marwood close, Piers had thought the timely thunder-clap might facilitate his task of proposing (for, of course, he had no choice but to do so now), but as he watched the white-gowned, golden-haired young lady walk calmly away from him towards the fireplace, he felt at a distinct disadvantage at having being cited as the cause of her fright.

Sophia was far from calm, though, and at once exclaimed, most uncharac-teristically, at the sad state of the fire. In the Marwood establishments fires usu-ally burned without any fostering from the family, but in this instance one had been caused to be lit in the drawing-room by Sir Ralph, somewhat late in the morning; with the added instruction that Miss Sophia and Mr Aubery were on no account to be interrupted. Dry kindling was a scarce commodity in such a wet year and even the army of Marwood servants had been defeated on this occasion — or almost: a whisp of smoke could still be seen.

'Can you not throw on another log, or resurrect it in some way?' Sophia asked, more for something to say than with any real interest in the wretched thing.

Piers, equally untutored in the secrets of fire-lighting, hurried forward to his companion. 'Yes, to be sure, ma'am.'

He picked up the fire-irons in a gingerly fashion, leaned across to the wood and too late recalled his tight coat. A button clinked onto the hearth with a sound, to his raw nerves as deafening as the thunder.

The two young people watched the button roll slowly and drunkenly towards Sophia: his gaze was one of suppressed fury and embarrassment; hers, simple amusement. When it came to rest in one final swerving turn Sophia snatched it up. (It was quite beyond Piers' power to bend so far to retrieve it without the danger of shedding a positive shower of its fellows.) She turned twinkling blue eyes upon his solemn face and chuckled, holding the offending button out to him in the palm of her hand.

Piers had little sense of humour, and in any event had less reason than usual for merriment that particular morning. 'Thank you, ma'am,' he said a trifle bleakly, then realising he might turn the incident to some purpose, went on with a sort of deperate gaiety: 'I am in a poor way, as you can see, for making a proposal of marriage — for sink to my knees I dare not!'

It was Sophia's turn to look serious, for although she had affected complete confidence in Mr Aubery's purpose in calling, she had been given no real reason for supposing he would seek her hand in marriage: in fact the small attentions he had paid to Emily had not gone unnoticed by her and she suspected he entertained a decided preference for her sister. Nor, of course, had she envisaged — in her countless daydreams — a betrothal scene of such brutal brevity from one usually given to urbane and flattering speeches. However, it was not over yet, she reflected, and made haste to encourage him. 'Are you trying to tell me you intend to propose to *me*?' she said archly.

Piers, by this time thoroughly nettled by his own ineptitude, replied stiffly, 'I am indeed, ma'am. I have this moment left your father, whose wishes I have naturally consulted on the matter, and now I humbly present myself to you for your decision.' Still turning the button between his slim fingers like a talisman, he concluded the formal petition by saying: 'Will you do me the honour of becoming my wife?'

It could not but be admitted that Sophia found her suitor sadly lacking in ardour and this, her first proposal, disappointing in the extreme; but nevertheless against all her expectations he *was* proposing to her, and perhaps these occasions were rather more starchy affairs than she had been led to expect. The depressing background of driving rain and intermittent thunder seemed to be at odds with the situation, too, she thought . . .

But, after only the briefest of pauses when Piers' hopes started to rise, she answered demurely: 'Yes, I will.' Then her enthusiasm could be suppressed no longer. 'Oh, I did so hope you would ask me! You see . . . ' She hesitated here, doubtful about the propriety of declaring her feelings before he should do so, but her open and ebullient nature triumphed. 'You see I have loved you from the first wonderful moment we met at the Exhibition.'

Piers felt compelled to meet the frank trusting gaze and that, together with the obviously sincere avowal, presented him with the worst facer yet. Dammit, he thought, if I'd known those were her sentiments I would have risked a dozen soakings rather than take the gamble: there had clearly been not the least chance in the world of her refusing his offer. But, as an assured gamester, he allowed no inkling of these reflections to appear in his greenish eyes; instead he smiled and raised her hand to his lips.

'You do me a great honour, ma'am. I had no idea your feelings were so deeply engaged.'

By the conclusion of this brief acknowledgement he had accepted that the die was cast and he must submit to his fate with a good grace. At once he started to calculate how best to exploit the situation — whilst his future bride waited hopefully for signs that her affections were reciprocated . . . She was disappointed again.

'When shall it be then, do you suppose?' he asked briskly, thinking that an early marriage would at least put the dibs in tune for a few months, and after that . . . Well, who knows? he thought, his naturally sanguine spirits rising: perhaps the Chelbeck Charger *would* make his fortune after all . . .

'The announcement of the betrothal, you mean?' Sophia's innocent eyes looked at him in a puzzled way under her long fair lashes.

'Why no! The date of the wedding! Is there any reason we should wait?'

Gratified by these first signs of eagerness, she replied quickly: 'None at all for my part, but what did papa say?' She could not believe there would be no setbacks: everything was working out just a little too smoothly — and swiftly — to be true.

'I fancy we did not set a date for what was — at that point — an uncertain event!'

His tone had reverted to the light, bantering one to which she was accustomed and she felt reassured. 'Papa raised no objections to the match?' she felt compelled to ask, all the same.

'Not one, as I remember!' he declared cheerfully enough, but could not suppress a moment's bitterness at recalling the total rejection of his initial choice of bride.

'Well than, shall we ask him?' Sophia saw his momentary abstraction. ' . . . About the date of the wedding?' she prompted. It was so hard to believe she was discussing this enormously important event in her life so matter-of-factly — just as if it were of no more significance than the date of her next singing lesson.

'Oh, certainly,' Piers agreed readily enough, but ran a hand through his coppery curls in a nervous fashion. Well, he thought, why not? He could not take his leave yet awhile, for the storm showed no sign of abating, and for the first time in his life he was at a loss to know what to say to a pretty girl.

Sophia, too, was not sorry to terminate the interview, although only ten minutes before, that sentiment would have amazed her. She consoled herself, however, by reflecting that when these formalities were concluded there would be many occasions in the future when they would be alone, and

Mr Aubery would surely be more demonstrative then.

* * *

After Sophia's departure, Emily and her Aunt Ashton were left to speculate upon Mr Aubery's presence in the house: they knew he had not left yet, and almost at once the storm broke preventing any but the doughtiest from venturing outdoors.

'I expect he is waiting for the weather to clear before he summons his carriage,' Mrs Ashton observed in gloomy tones, setting aside her sewing after nervously dropping her needle at the first flash of lightning.

'Yes, I am persuaded he is,' Emily corroborated cheerfully. 'Papa will be cross! He was not in very plump currant this morning to begin with, and a prolonged visit will set up his bristles!'

'Really, what a way to refer to your poor papa,' Mrs Ashton said mechanically, her attention on the storm.

After the shattering overhead clap of thunder, she rose to her feet and announced in tremulous tones: 'I will go and lie down for a while, I think. Storms always give me the headache.'

'Yes, of course.' Emily knew her aunt had a great dislike of thunder and lightning, but wished she had not left at that particular moment: she was still apprehensive that Mr Aubery might suddenly be shown in to her, should her papa tire of his company.

The purpose of his visit was still obscure but she was prey to the strongest sensation that he intended to offer for her. What if her papa should forget her particular wishes in the matter? There was no doubt he was becoming more absentminded as every day passed . . .

With the worst tension of the storm released in the steady downpour of rain, she quit pacing the room and snatched up Sophia's marble-covered book — one of the sentimental effusions of the Minerva Press, upon

which her young sister feasted whenever they came up to town: for when
they were fixed at Hollsted her papa
forbade the ordering, through the
carrier, of such trashy novels from
Hookham's Library; but during their
sojourn in London Sophia was free to
select anything she wished merely by
calling in person at the Library
premises in Bond Street. All of which
was a fair example of Sir Ralph's
haphazard disciplining of his younger
daughter, thought Emily, who lost a
vast amount of sleep because of this
particular circumstance. For on occasion Sophia had the candle burning
long after midnight, devouring as many
volumes as she could before their
return into the country.

She persisted with the first pages of
the novel for some time, but her lack of
concentration was made apparent to
her when she realised at last it was
volume two she had picked up. Setting
it aside crossly she made herself sit
quite unoccupied for a while, merely

watching the rain coursing down the window panes. However, when Sophia still did not return, and she was increasingly conscious of Mr Aubery's unsettling proximity somewhere, she rose abruptly and decided to see how her aunt went on.

She was scarcely across the threshold into the hall when she regretted her action, for advancing towards her was her papa, leaning heavily on his stick and Mr Aubery's arm, with Sophia — an amazingly solemn-looking Sophia — by their visitor's side.

'Ah, my dear Emily! How very fortuitous!' cried Sir Ralph exultantly. 'You shall be the first to hear the happy news, as you should be!'

His choice of words could not have been more at odds with the expressions of his young companions: Emily was totally baffled, and scarcely less so when she perceived Mr Aubery cast a mournful, almost accusatory glance in her direction when he first caught sight of her.

She murmured a greeting to him, then said: 'Well, papa, some cheerful news will not come amiss on this dreary day!' The only explanation she could imagine was that he *had* bought Mr Aubery's collection of paintings after all, and at a price which gladdened her parent's heart and had cast the vendor into the sullens. Consequently, the real reason, promptly divulged, came as a shock.

She was aware her features must have registered dismay, and very quickly she endeavoured to recover herself. 'Forgive me! I own the news has taken me completely by surprise!' But she found she could not bring herself to express formal phrases of congratulation and pleasure when the protagonists were scowling so! 'You are surely not leaving, Mr Aubery?' she asked, as he seemed to be edging his way uneasily to the street door. 'Could you not stay and take dinner with us?'

'That is most kind of you, Miss Marwood,' he said, in tones of cold punctilio, as if he had never seen her before — which was in complete contrast to his earlier manner towards her and hardly commensurate in one destined to be her brother-in-law. 'I fear I have plagued Sir Ralph quite enough for one day. And there does seem to be a lull in the storm, too. It may not be of long duration,' he concluded feebly.

'Ay, we are all at the mercy of the elements!' Sir Ralph commented with some feeling.

During this exchange, and while Mr Aubery donned his driving gloves — and a cloak which had been sent in to him by his brother's much maligned tiger, Judd, who was waiting with the curricle — Emily tried to intercept Sophia's gaze, but she was doing her utmost to avoid looking in her direction. A brief smile had flickered across Sophia's face when Sir Ralph made his initial announcement, but scarcely the expression of joy unbounded which Emily would have anticipated from her in the circumstances. She had, after all, achieved her dearest ambition, presumably, so why the almost woebegone air?

Emily discovered the answer from her sister when she went up to their room to change for dinner. For the past two hours Emily had been frustrated for enlightment, for Sir Ralph had immediately taken his rest after Mr Aubery's departure, and Sophia had made it plain she did not want to speak to anyone. However, she had little choice but to do so now — or at least until Brice, their maid, should arrive.

Sophia was standing by the bedroom window. She was scarcely admiring the view, though, for their room only overlooked a small courtyard and the rickety tiled roofs of some stables — which had gleamed wetly almost every day since their arrival: nonetheless she did not turn around when her sister spoke to her.

'Sophia? I had thought you must be overjoyed . . . Why so dismal when you have achieved your dearest wish?'

But — as is often the case with things

which are greatly desired — now it had been granted it was not the untrammelled joy anticipated.

'I haven't — not yet,' Sophia said morosely. 'Papa says we must wait a year before we marry. A *year!*' she cried in disgust, having forgotten already, apparently, that only a few hours before she had never really expected to become Mrs Aubery at all.

Emily was relieved to hear of this delay, and she said assuagingly: 'But that is a perfectly reasonable stipulation on papa's part, you must see!'

'No, I cannot! And nor can Mr Aubery, I fancy! He was most anxious we should be wed as soon as possible.' She turned abruptly to face her sister, her blonde ringlets fanning out. ' — And so am I'

Was he, indeed? thought Emily with swift suspicion. 'You must bear in mind you will acquire a considerable sum of money in your own right when you are twenty-five — papa is quite right to be prudent about the man you are to marry . . . You haven't mentioned the existence of this fortune to Mr Aubery before, have you?'

'Of course I have not! We do not regard the stupid money! We love each other and want to marry, that is all! Can't you understand?' she said contemptuously.

Brice arrived before Emily could attempt to answer this taunt, and she hazarded that the maid would not be a party to the news as yet: the butler knew, of course, but Twell would hardly be inclined to share these momentous tidings with his minions — he was both autocratic and secretive. Luckily the storm was uppermost in Brice's mind and, as she had just come from administering lavender drops to Mrs Ashton, she was under the impression that the weather had provided the most stirring event that day.

Both girls were happy to leave the vexed question of Sophia's betrothal for the moment, but Emily resolved to tax her father with the matter as soon as she could. She misliked the sound of the Hon. Piers Aubery more and more as a prospective husband for Sophia, and perhaps there was still a chance she could influence her parent's decision. In doing so she realized she must jeopardize her relationship with her sister, as well as perhaps causing her to fly in all their faces by eloping.

There was an additional factor, too, in that Emily's confidence in being able to judge Mr Aubery's character was ebbing: first of all, she felt somewhat chastened to discover that he, far from forming an attachment for her as she thought, had actually been on the verge of proposing to her sister; secondly, the much-maligned Aunt Ashton had been more accurate in *her* estimation of the gentleman and his intentions than she had herself . . .

Emily was left with a purely inst-inctive apprenhesion of a certain unsteadiness in Mr Aubery's character and an eagerness of mind which hinted at a sad lack of caution. However, although a long talk with her father did nothing to substantiate these impressions (indeed, he seemed to be won over by these self-same tendencies, which he designated ambition and enterprise) nonetheless she remained unconvinced. In voicing criticism of Mr Aubery she found herself quite alone in their household, for everyone from Sir Ralph down to Jenny was loud in his praises.

The year's wait which Sir Ralph had imposed upon the couple, stemmed, Emily discovered, from no particular caution in regard to Mr Aubery: it was simply, he maintained, what he would have asked of any prospective bridegroom in the circumstances.

' . . . For I cannot see what reason there is for haste in the matter,' he explained. 'And in a year their house can be made ready for them at Hollsted. Besides, these things take time,' he went on a trifle irritably, his leg still paining him. 'There are lawyers to see, settlements to be drawn up and, in any event, it will give my little Sophia all the time in the world to prepare for a most splendid wedding.' His eyes glinted briefly with pleasure. 'That is what you young ladies like, is it not?

'This way she will be presented next spring, as we had planned, and married soon after . . . Everything in its due course, eh, my dear? And who knows, perhaps you will be settled by then, also?' he concluded optimistically, still anxious above all things to have all conform to his rigid idea of etiquette.

It was no use, Emily knew, trying to convince her papa — who had stoically survived four years of legal wrangling before his own marriage — that that was not how the two impatient young people would view the matter. He would retort that if their feelings were not constant enough to face a year's betrothal they should not embark upon marriage at all: a conclusion with which she agreed wholeheartedly — if for different reasons.

No mention was made at that point

of the official announcement of the betrothal, but it was not long before Mrs Ashton was pressing for the matter to be made public so that she (or rather, Emily) could organise a celebratory dance.

It was then that Emily decided she must seek advice outside the circle of her family, and where else to start but with the Auberys? She dealt well with Harriet, although had never paid a morning-visit to her unaccompanied before: now she determined to do so, if only to discover how Mr Aubery's family viewed the match.

9

'You didn't take a soaking in the storm yesterday, then?' Roland asked his young brother casually as they rode side by side along Savile Row.

'You know damn well I didn't, for Judd has told you, I'll be bound!' he grinned.

'Indeed, he has not!' Not in so many words, in any event, reflected Roland; but what his man told him was that young Master Piers had been at the Marwoods' residence an unconscionable time during that tempestuous morning. Following which Judd and the curricle had not been dismissed by Piers until the early evening; and by then the disgruntled servant had been only too ready to complain to his master, Roland, about his irksome day.

'Well, since I am in the best of good humours, I shall not resent your fraternal curiosity this time.'

'That's mighty condescending of you! But then I daresay you'll not satisfy it, either!'

'*Au contraire!*' Piers responded, touching his hat with the whip in a most gracious manner, as they halted at a corner to allow a girl selling watercresses to cross. They turned into Glass House Street and he continued: 'I have every intention of explaining the reason for my extreme cheer.'

'Oh? I thought that was due to this visit to Long Acre to see your precious Charger.'

'Dear me, no! Although that *is* very gratifying, of course, it can no longer take pride of place in my interests henceforth.'

'Piers!' Roland cried, assuming the ominous look which Harriet so dreaded when the brothers quarrelled. 'You are not, I trust, trying to tell me you have undertaken yet *another* scheme, for if you have, I make no bones about it, I shall — !'

'Hold hard, you'll have a fit of the apoplexy! Perhaps my words were a trifle ill-chosen, but I meant only to convey that congratulations are quite in order — I am to be married, you see.' There was no doubt that Piers always enjoyed teasing and taunting his brother, and he was more than satisfied with the effect this disclosure had upon him.

Roland eyed him with a look of total disbelief. 'That cannot be so! Why, only a couple of weeks ago you denied all interest in the married state.'

'Not I!' he exclaimed indignantly. 'I trust you do not suggest I have acted in an underhand fashion! Only two *days* ago I asked you about the settlement due on my marriage.'

'Yes, yes, so you did,' Roland agreed, confused — and alarmed. 'Who is it?' he asked baldly.

'The lady of my choice,' Piers announced repressively, but with an unhappy turn of phrase all things considered, 'is Miss Sophia Marwood.'

'Sophia?' Roland echoed. 'Not the elder sister — Miss Marwood?'

'No dammit! Why should it be?' He was genuinely upset now, for Roly had touched upon a very sore spot indeed.

'No reason at all,' Roland said mildly, surprised by his vehemence. 'Except it did appear at one point that you and Ned might be vying for her affections, but clearly I was mistaken.'

'Not entirely, where Ned is concerned,' Piers said in bitter tones, 'for Miss Marwood, I collect, is most likely already promised to him.'

'To Ned?' cried Roland, who seemed even more startled by this revelation than the earlier one.

Piers was irritated by this unwelcome diversion. 'Well, I was given to understand she is promised to *someone* and, as you remarked yourself, Ned was making a cake of himself over her,' he observed caustically. 'Ergo, it does not take too much brilliance of thought to conclude it is he . . . However, since his affairs appear to command your interest more than do mine, perhaps you'd like to ask him about it at Long Acre when we get there.'

Roland glanced again at his brother in surprise. 'You've asked him over to see the coach this morning?'

'Why not?'

Piers had wanted Ned there so that his brother should not be able to ask too many probing questions about the cost of the work being done on the vehicle. But he had issued the invitation before seeing Sir Ralph, and he was not looking forward to meeting Ned now: they were never on a very cordial footing — Piers being well aware that Ned regarded him as frivolous, even worthless fellow. Of one thing he was certain, he would get but short shrift from Ned if *he* were his elder brother and not Roly.

'No, no reason, I had thought this was a family viewing of the Charger, that is all.' Roland commented, without particular concern.

'Well, he *was* almost family, wasn't

he?' Piers said morosely, wishing for the first time that Ned had married Harriet all those years ago.

But Roland did not intend to embark upon that subject with Piers: he had resolved to approach Ned on Harriet's behalf after her impassioned outburst, but now — well, it was too late, obviously. Nor would he consider broaching the question of Miss Marwood with him either, as Piers had suggested: he had had his fill already of his brief foray into matchmaking. If Piers married a Marwood he would be satisfied with that . . .

'I'm sorry if I seem insensible to your momentous news but you have chosen a somewhat fraught occasion to tell me!' he said, shouting, and not for the first time, above the grind and rattle of a passing carriage. 'But I am delighted! Truly, I think you are a lucky fellow!' He knew none of the details, of course, but he could not but be pleased that his young brother would soon be settled; besides, from the little he knew of her, he thought Miss Sophia to be much better suited to Piers than Miss Marwood could ever be — they would make a lively pair!

Piers, who was genuinely becoming used to the prospect of his unexpected future wife, and was prepared to make the best of the situation, explained he had chosen that moment to tell him because he would be from home a good deal now supervising the launching of the Charger. ' . . . And, I daresay Sir Ralph's man of law will be approaching you soon, and I want you to be well-prepared!' He had, in fact, elected to tell Roly in this way so that he should not be at once questioned too deeply on the matter: he wanted time to think, and to devise some scheme for either advancing the date of the marriage, or for acquiring some of the monies involved before the end of the year — indeed, before the end of the month was his aim. As there was little chance of his prising any ready rhino out of Sir Ralph, a starchy old-stickler if ever he saw one, he would have to dig some out of Roly again — which wouldn't be easy . . . Still, he would think of some shift or other, he always did.

'That's not my concern,' said Roland with some relief. 'I will refer Sir Ralph's man to Henfield who will know how to go on.'

The devil he will, thought Piers; and once those two dry old coves get their craggy heads together I'll be lucky to be wed in time to see the thirty thousand pounds . . . when was it? He *must* find out how old the girl was!

'Shall you tell Ned your news, this morning?' Roland asked.

'Damned if I know . . . Best not to, I suppose, but I don't know the order of the day in these affairs. Leave it to the ladies, I daresay: they'll soon blazon it all over town! Bye the bye — how old is Sophia Marwood, do you suppose?'

Roland laughed. 'How should I know? But she doesn't look above sixteen to me.'

'My God, you're not serious, are

you?' he cried, aghast.

'If you've got Sir Ralph's blessing, what difference does it make? You're not Methuselah!'

'Oh, not the least in the world,' Piers replied airily, deciding he had said enough on the matter: there was no call to rouse his brother's suspicions of his motives already. Not that he could prevent his marrying where he wished, but he might get some high-minded notion it was his duty to tell Sir Ralph a few details of his financial escapades: one could never tell with Roly when he got the bit between his teeth . . . 'See you at Long Acre!' he cried suddenly, spurring his horse.

Roland, well-used to Piers' inability to hold to one subject or interest, however important, for any time at all, glanced up at the street sign which read Knaves' Acre, smiled ruefully, and made a determined effort to overtake his younger brother . . .

He succeeded only because Piers had encountered Ned, also on the way to the coachmaker's, and already the talk was fixed upon the safe subject of carriages.

The vehicle, which was destined to blazon the name Chelbeck across the land, looked far from impressive, for it was bereft of wheels but had already assumed its regal colour; and artisans seemed to be swarming all over it — a currier, lamp-maker, trimmer and even a herald painter were in attendance.

Roland learned that three more coats of copal varnish would see the body-work finished, and that the elliptical springs were the finest available, but could find no one in attendance at the workshop to reassure him that all these splendours would be provided within the costs quoted to him. To his untutored eye it seemed unlikely, but then he had seen the estimates, and it was not the time to cavil when Piers was showing off his new possession so proudly to Ned and himself.

So Piers was able to breathe a sigh of relief as they left the coachmaker's. The three men rode together for a short distance then Piers took his leave, saying: 'Don't fret, Roly, if you don't see me at Bittadon House for the next few days! I shall be riding the Dover Road sweetening up the bonifaces en route — I need to have dinner served, by one of them in less than a pig's whisper for my post-haste travellers!'

Roland and Ned continued on their way in a staid-seeming silence after their companion's voluble departure.

'What do you think of my madcap brother's latest scheme, Ned?' Roland said at last.

'Well, if he can maintain this level of enthusiasm it can scarcely fail, can it?' his friend replied diplomatically, his lean brown face impassive.

'Come now, you know Piers! Do you think it can be a profitable affair?'

'Profitable?' The impassivity gave way to incredulity. 'I should beg leave to doubt that if the lavish style of that coach is anything to judge by! But surely it is just one of Piers' hobby-horses, is it not?'

'Oh — yes . . . yes, of course,' agreed Roland hastily, but given pause to think by the response — which confirmed his own growing doubts. 'We haven't seen you of late at Bittadon House,' he said, changing the subject.

'No, and I'm afraid I must ride into Northamptonshire in a few days. There are various pressing matters about the estate for my attention, and this damnable weather doesn't improve anything, does it? Are there any commissions I can carry out for you whilst I am there?'

'Yes, you may call at Chelbeck and tell Beechers to stop bombarding me with his lugubrious letters — if I am not prepared for ruination now, I never will be!' Then he went on, in more serious vein, 'No, thank you, there is nothing. My bailiff is mournful but efficient. I shall stay fixed comfortably in town until July, I fancy.'

As intended this remark made Ned seek to justify his own precipitate return into the country. 'I wish I could do likewise but there are some property repairs I must oversee.'

This did not tell Roland very much, any more than his parting remark did. 'Give my best compliments to your sister,' he said, making his only reference to Harriet that morning.

All in all Roland had been furnished with some disturbing intelligence, but Piers' betrothal at least was welcome news.

Harriet, when she was told of it by her twin, was a little disappointed: like Roland she had thought Piers' choice would fall on Emily. However, Roland did not pass on the surmise — for it was not more than that, he kept telling himself — that Miss Marwood was already promised to Ned. Piers, though, on one of his fleeting visits home a few days later, casually rectified this omission; and Harriet was still stunned by the news when Emily's call was announced a half hour later.

It was more than she could do at that

moment to face Emily, and regretfully she had herself denied.

When Peck told Emily that Harriet was out she felt quite despairing: the past few days had been lonely ones for her as she fretted over her sister's future whilst all about her rejoiced, and now she was prevented from even discussing it with someone else — who might perhaps reassure her . . .

Lord Bittadon was crossing the hall and he came to greet her.

'How kind of you to call, Miss Marwood: Harriet will be pleased to see you,' he said affably.

Peck intervened at once with a speaking look at his master. 'I have just ascertained that Miss Aubery is from home, my lord.'

'That's a great pity,' Roland commented, whilst he wondered what possessed his sister to refuse to see a visitor: it was so unlike her. Then, simultaneously with deciding *he* would like to talk to Miss Marwood, in the hope of discovering some hint about her relationship with Ned, it occurred to him that that indeed might be the reason Harriet did *not* want to see her. That wretch Piers must have let slip something of it to her: Roland had not remembered to warn him to keep his suspicions to himself.

'Perhaps you would care to wait awhile? I daresay Harriet may return at any time — and if you do not object to bearing me company meanwhile?' Roland offered.

Emily grasped at this straw for, although she would not have thought of approaching Lord Bittadon on the forth-coming marriage, he would have more influence, surely, over his young brother than would Harriet.

Roland led her into the book-room — an amazingly snug room, thought Emily, in a house which also contained the vast and impressive Louis Quatorze salon and the picture-gallery. How long ago it seemed since their first visit, but in fact it was scarcely two months.

'Forgive the disarray,' Roland said,

indicating his desk strewn about with papers. 'Has my brother told you of the Chelbeck Charger?' He removed a map of Kent from a chair so that his visitor could be seated.

Emily stared at her host. 'I don't believe so ... What is it — a race-horse?'

Roland laughed: the first time he had done so in recent days over this vexed subject. 'Would that it were! No, this seems to be the equivalent of a good many race horses — in expense at any rate,' he said with feeling. 'It is the name of his precious stage-coach!'

'Oh yes, he did say something about it, I recall.'

Emily sounded unenthusiastic because she inevitably associated it with the embarrassing conversation she had had with Mr Aubery, but Roland thought she was perhaps disapproving of the venture. He hoped it would not jeopardize the forthcoming connexion between the two families.

'Well, it promises to be the most

sumptuous vehicle on the Dover Road, I can tell you that!'

'The Dover Road? Our Hollsted land borders that route so your brother will be very conveniently placed indeed, will he not?'

'I'm sorry? How so?'

Emily's heart sank: had Mr Aubery said nothing to the family of his plans? Well, if she were to gain anything from this visit they had to be told. If it were a clandestine arrangement, all the better — perhaps it could be stopped at once. 'Why, you must know, it is proposed that my sister and he should have a house at Hollsted when they are wed.'

'Er — no, I did not,' Roland admitted reluctantly, feeling a trifle handicapped by his ignorance: however, if he could not discover anything about Ned and this young lady, at least he could perhaps acquire some valuable information about his own brother! 'I have heard no details of their plans as yet, although my sister and I were delighted to hear of the match, of course.'

Here was a chance, thought Emily, to air her misgivings, but dare she do so . . . ?

Roland was quick to sense her hesitation. 'And you are not so delighted . . . Am I right?'

She blessed him silently for his perception and found courage to say: 'Frankly, I am not, my lord. Oh, do not misunderstand me, my doubts centre upon my sister. You cannot know what a worry it is to have the well-being of someone dear to you at heart, and to see them acting foolishly beyond permission — and on a matter of such magnitude!' she burst out passionately.

'I would not be too sure of that, Miss Marwood,' he said in quiet and heart-felt tones.

She saw the look of understanding in the gentle grey eyes and suddenly felt that here, at last, was someone to whom she could unburden her anxieties. Needing no further encouragement, she told him of her good but occasionally misguided parent, her flighty sister, and her well-meaning but totally ineffective aunt-chaperon.

'Who is the very antithesis of Aunt Knowle, I collect! Now, there's a lady who could impose some discipline for you!' cried Roland. 'You may not know, but Harriet and I are not the only twins in our family — there are two younger sisters, both safely married now — I thank heaven! Although, I should give thanks to Aunt Knowle who drove them through the hazards of the marriage mart with the same vigilance and persistence with which a whipper-in drives his hounds!'

'I feel sure from what I know of the lady she would greatly relish the comparison!' Emily said, lifted out of her depression momentarily by this diverting picture.

'Yes, indeed! Her curious idiomatic manner of speech upsets the sensibilities of the more fastidious, I fear, but was invaluable for putting to rout unwelcome suitors, I may say! Harriet and I are forever indebted to her for acting chaperon to Augusta and Helen.'

Emily wondered fleetingly if Ned Grimsby had been put to rout, though, by the same alarming lady.

As Roland described some of the additional difficulties Aunt Knowle had encountered in steering identical sisters towards eligible marriage partners, he noticed for the first time the quite startingly blue eyes of his listener, and also the fine-boned face and fair complexion. Why had he not realized before that she was really quite beautiful? The answer was that he had been too preoccupied trying either to hurl her in his brother's path or to steer her from Ned's. Lord yes, he must attempt to find out about Ned . . .

Emily was aware of his searching look, and in the brief silence which followed his entertaining tales she said: 'I don't know why I have troubled you with my fears — I cannot expect you, of all people, to dissuade my sister — or your own brother — from the course they have chosen!'

'Well, no, I don't believe I can help you in any direct fashion,' he agreed, but in tones of great sympathy. 'My brother is of age and is in no way at my command.' (Which was only too true, he thought ruefully; he was as effective in controlling Piers' mad starts as Miss Marwood evidently was in restraining her sister.)

Emily immediately confirmed this. 'And my sister although *not* of age is certainly not at my command!' she declared. 'Papa is too easily swayed by Sophia's volatile wishes, but I *know* she is much too immature to form a lasting attachment,' she said vehemently.

'Might I enquire how old your sister is?' Roland interposed swiftly, remembering Piers' inexplicable enquiry.

'Eighteen, but her youthful appearance and tomboyish ways argue strongly against it being so. However, I do not believe anything will convince papa that Sophia could be mistaken in her feelings for a gentleman who has so much in his favour as Mr Aubery has — as well as holding high Tory principles, I collect, which are so dear to papa's heart!' Feeling now she had said more than enough on the matter to the brother of the gentleman in question, she concluded on a light-hearted note: 'No one could accuse Sophia of being motivated by anything but the highest *romantical* principles — she does not care one rush for politics, or even his paintings, be they by Claude or Poussin! A dashing stage-coach, I must own, might carry more influence with her!'

Roland was endeavouring to puzzle out exactly what it was that Sir Ralph saw in Piers' favour, when he was completely floored by his visitor's reference to the paintings.

His deepening frown convinced Emily she had overstayed her welcome.

'Please, ma'am, don't go! Forgive my doltish expression but it never occurred to me that my brother nurtured any political — let alone Tory principles!' He had been present, of course, when Sir Ralph had somehow misconstrued Piers' remarks about Byron and had transposed him into a Tory, but in what else had Sir Ralph subsequently been mistaken? — or even actively misled, perhaps? It seemed, in any event, that Piers might have laid claim to the picture collection, and anxious though Roland had been to be spared the intricacies of the marriage settlement, he felt he must concern himself now.

However, he gave no hint of this to his visitor, of course, and Emily was unaware that she had achieved anything with her call.

So, she felt rather disheartened as she protested: 'I must leave, for I have no right to impose upon your time in this way, my lord. But I am indebted to you for bearing with my apprehensions — which I daresay will prove to be much cry and little wool!'

'Let us hope so,' he said, trying to be heartening. 'Oh, and can you enlighten me on the date of the forthcoming nuptials? I should not care to miss them!'

'You need entertain no fears on that head! Papa has decreed they must wait a year.'

'A year!' Good lord, he thought, Piers has never held to an idea for more than a month, let alone twelve! He was surprised, too, that his brother had seemed so happy with the situation: was he then already up to some fetch or other with the Marwoods?

'You sound as appalled as my sister at the prospect,' said Emily with a smile. 'But papa is a prodigious stickler, and this way Sophia can be presented next spring as planned, and I could be settled, too — so all would be meet and fitting!'

Well, he thought, it was the only opportunity he was likely to be given to discover Miss Marwood's own plans, so he seized at it. 'And will all be meet and fitting, do you suppose?'

'Who can say?' was the unsatisfactory

response. 'However, I confess my prime fear is that they — but enough of my fears and fancies,' she said briskly, realizing she had been about to cast Lord Bittadon's brother in the role of abductor. She had already said enough, and to no great purpose, she felt.

But there she was wrong: Roland divined very quickly that *her* prime fear evidently coincided with his own; after all, he had more reason for apprehending an elopement — given the circumstances and his special knowledge of Piers.

'Miss Marwood,' he said, as they awaited Peck to show her out, 'Pray do not feel you have been on a sleeveless errand, for I believe that to be far from the case. As I intimated, I cannot order my brother where to marry — indeed, any interference would confirm his resolve, I daresay, but there may be influences I can bring to bear . . .'

Which is all very well, she thought impatiently, but will it be in time to prevent them eloping?

' . . . And, depend upon it, I am well aware there may not be all the time in the world at my disposal.'

She could have flung her arms about his neck with relief on hearing this confirmation that he really did understand the nature of her anxieties, but Peck's arrival depressed any such unseemly display: as it was, the man made plain his disapproval of this tête-à-tête by permitting himself a rare look of censure at his master.

His lordship, however, had matters of greater moment to concern him: three to be exact, and he considered disaster might well ensue if any one of them was neglected.

10

The unexpected, private talk which Lord Bittadon had with Miss Marwood was destined to have a profound influence upon him: already he had altered his opinion of Piers' marriage — not for any more specific reason, though, than that he knew his brother would never endure a year's waiting for *anything*. Whilst shying from designating Piers a gazetted fortune-hunter he knew the lady's dowry — whatever its size — would be a prime influence with him. It was also clear to Roland that, if Piers had made false claims for his own fortune and property, the marriage settlement would never be signed by Sir Ralph. But Piers, by trying to thrust the responsibility for the drawing up of the settlement on to Roland, had given every appearance of indifference to the financial and legal aspect of the marriage . . . The more Roland thought about it the more he was convinced that elopement would be in his brother's mind: for if it were accomplished early enough, Sir Ralph's permission would not be revoked by then; the betrothal would have been made public; and the young lady herself would, it seemed, be unlikely to hesitate.

Of the three matters needing his attention, Lord Bittadon reckoned this to be the most urgent, depending as it did upon his brother's volatile disposition and involving the possible ruination of an innocent young lady: another of his anxieties also concerned his brother — this time with the Chelbeck Charger — but as that affair encompassed only his own partial financial ruination Roland placed it second in priority: the third problem, his perennial worry about Harriet and Ned, he decided could wait awhile, as a note to Mrs Grimsby had ascertained that Ned was to continue out of town for a week or more yet.

In making the latter assumption he miscalculated badly, as he discovered when, about a week later, he rode over to the house in Clarges Street which Ned and his mother had rented for the season.

Mrs Grimsby received him with an apology. 'I'm so sorry, but Ned is not returned yet, my lord,' she said, as she darted hesitantly about the parlour like a chaffinch, twitching a cushion here and fractionally moving an ornament there. 'Is your business with him of an urgent nature?'

'Urgent, yes ma'am, I believe it may be, but it was you I called to see this morning.'

She came to a halt and fixed him with her bird-bright eyes. 'Oh! Well then, please take a seat, my lord.' He did tower above one, she found, and he was so much broader built than Ned. But Mrs Grimsby had always liked the open nature and gentle disposition of young Lord Bittadon, although since his twin sister's utter rejection of her son she had experienced a little uneasiness with the Auberys: it was Ned's wish they should all go on as before, though, and she had done all she could to conceal this feeling for his sake. However, she was aware that the time might be approaching now when their connexion with the Auberys might wither naturally if, indeed, it did not suffer a direct cut.

'You are not, I take it, in immediate expectation of Ned's return, ma'am?' Roland enquired, as the last thing he wanted was the arrival of his friend during this particularly delicate discussion.

'Would that I were! No, I have no notion when precisely he intends to quit Northamptonshire.'

At mention of their shared native county the conversation turned to mutual local acquaintances for a space. However, Mrs Grimsby knew Lord Bittadon had not called to gossip about their neighbours — and told him so.

'Yes, you are quite right, ma'am,'

Roland agreed, grateful for the opening to a difficult subject. 'I confess I have shirked making a push on this particular matter for a long time, but I feel now there is nothing to be lost by approaching you. To put it bluntly, I have only recently discovered how matters stand between Harriet and your son: and I wondered if you were privy to Ned's sentiments after my twin's rejection of his suit?'

'Yes, I believe I know them very well,' she said quietly, then went on in brisker tones: 'But I own it surprises me to hear that you have only *now* discovered the way things stand: I had imagined, I suppose, that twins must know each other's thoughts instinctively — perhaps even more than mothers and sons,' she concluded with a faint smile.

Roland smiled too, but his expression was of a rueful nature. 'After eight-and-twenty years as Harriet's twin I laboured under the same illusion, but this has proved me to be sadly in error!' There was a brief silence, and it became clear that Mrs Grimsby was not going to expand on her son's feelings without further prompting. 'However, her happiness is still of the deepest concern to me, and I hope you do not judge me to be treading in territory where I have no right, when I ask about Ned's attitude?'

'Indeed, no' Mrs Grimsby returned, with just a hint of brusqueness, 'but frankly I fear it is a trifle late now to be discussing it.'

'Oh, I see,' Roland said in depressed tones, his worst fears confirmed.

Observing the genuine unhappiness in his eyes, Mrs Grimsby relented a little. 'I, too, am far from content the way things have fallen out between your sister and Ned, but it was Harriet's decision, and if Ned can weather his very deep disappointment I must help him to do so . . . I do not scruple to say, however, I was quite stunned at Harriet's answer — so incomprehensible after all those years! Well, there it is! I did offer tentatively to have a quiet word with the girl for Ned, for I know she has sadly lacked the particular guidance of a mother these many years,' she said pointedly. 'But Ned would have none of it! And I believe he was right — it doesn't pay to meddle.'

Her visitor looked suitably shame-faced.

' . . . Oh, I do not mean you, my lord, but mothers and sons, you understand.' She gazed at him for a moment. 'But why do you approach me now?'

'Because when Harriet owned to me so belatedly what answer she had given to Ned, I gained the strong conviction that she has since come to regret it very deeply. They are so clearly at an impasse, ma'am! She can say nothing, and Ned is scarcely going to propose yet again after a repulse of that nature!'

Mrs Grimsby's small mouth had set in a firm line during this speech, and when finally she spoke it was clear she was disapproving. 'I do not know Harriet's reasons for her extraordinary behaviour, of course, but I *do* know my son has suffered quite dreadfully these past months. Oh, he says but little — you know Ned, it is not his way — nonetheless the hurt went deep: and now you appear! Just when he has met someone else and the scars are beginning to heal at last.'

By this time Roland was quite overcome with despondency and guilt: he should have known that even the usually mild Mrs Grimsby would defend her young like an outraged broody hen. Why hadn't he taken courage to approach Ned himself before?

When her visitor seemed disinclined to offer any comment, Mrs Grimsby went on in warning tones: 'I would not want anything to mar my son's chance of happiness now, you must see that. He is past thirty, you know, and the poor boy spent so many of his early years abroad . . . I daresay you will know who it is he has in mind without my telling you. She is a young lady very like Harriet in many ways, as I pointed out to Ned, and I believe them to be admirably suited to each other.'

In spite of his gloom, Roland was much struck by this perceptive remark. Miss Marwood *was* like Harriet, it was true: not in appearance to any degree, but their temperaments bore many similarities.

He sighed.

'Yes, I believe I know the lady — indeed Ned's attentions to her had not escaped my notice, and I suppose I was galvanized into acting largely because of that circumstance.'

'As I said, my lord, it is too late,' Mrs Grimsby reiterated firmly, and the small mouth snapped shut.

'Well, I cannot help wishing I *had* been apprised of this unhappy business earlier. I fancy I would have meddled then with all my might!' he told her with a sardonic laugh. However, he thought to himself, perhaps he could still meddle to some purpose? Presumably Ned had not actually committed himself to Miss Marwood as yet . . .

But Mrs Grimsby did not smile back

at this rather grim sally and, as if she were aware of his thoughts, said: 'I'm sorry you will not be seeing Ned for a while, and I shall have no means of letting you know when he returns, for I have promised to travel down to Portsmouth before the end of the week.'

'Ah yes, I see, ma'am,' said Roland, feeling quite routed by this sharp little woman.

As her visitor rose to go Mrs Grimsby could not resist adding: 'Mrs Ashton — Sir Ralph Marwood's sister, you know — kindly invited me to go with her to Portsmouth. Her son's ship is due to put in there in the near future, it seems, and she is quite determined to be on the quay to greet him, of course,' she concluded, suggesting what a sterling and indispensable band mothers were.

Roland departed from Clarges Street feeling a very unsterling and dispensable brother indeed. There was no gainsaying the fact that he had failed signally to exercise any beneficial influence on Harriet's or Piers' future. A reflection which served to remind him of his equally fruitless efforts, earlier that week, to impose some sort of order on his brother's affairs.

When he had approached Henfield about the marriage settlement the lawyer said he had heard nothing from Sir Ralph as yet, and, until he did, it was impossible to know what money and moveables had been pledged to the Marwoods by Piers. Roland left Henfield in no doubt as to the precise extent of Piers' entitlement, but no further action could be taken until the two parties consulted with each other. Roland had no wish to precipitate matters, however, so he directed the lawyer to await Sir Ralph's instructions.

As to the affair of the Chelbeck Charger, he was met with frustration at every turn: for the first time in his life it seemed that Piers had not yoked his noble brother with direct responsibility for paying his bills. Every tradesman whom Roland approached was quite adamant about the inviolability and secrecy of his arrangement with Mr Aubery — so much so that Roland's suspicion that something smoky was afoot increased ten-fold . . .

Now, as he rode disconsolately homewards, he felt his call on Mrs Grimsby had completed a singularly unprofitable week. All the admirable resolves formed after Miss Marwood's visit had come to nought, and now he had the prospect of facing his sister, knowing that their fears about Ned — hitherto stoutly denied by Roland — were true. Harriet had put a brave face on it, after her initial inability to confront Emily (a fact which had not been referred to by either twin since), and Roland was not going to disturb her fragile peace of mind further until the match was public knowledge, and could be denied no longer.

In happier days Harriet and Roland had often dined in comparative silence

— but it was the silence of understanding and the total absence of the need for small talk. Now there was often a strained and uncomfortable atmosphere. Roland was especially conscious of it the evening after his visit to Ned's mother.

'Has Piers been home today?' he asked, although even the escapades of his young brother were no longer the common ground they used to be between the twins: he had not divulged his suspicions to Harriet over the expenditure on the coach, or the possible duplicity over the marriage. The latter he could not mention because Harriet knew nothing of his talk with Miss Marwood.

'No,' replied Harriet, with an effort at brightness, and glad to seize upon any topic. 'Until he has this wretched coach on the road I doubt anyone will see a great deal of him!'

'Well, if he does condescend to cross the threshold, convey my regards, and tell him I'd like a word with him.'

On hearing the curt and sardonic tones she frowned across the polished table at her twin. 'I thought now that he has this new venture to occupy him, and his marriage plans fixed, he would cease to worry you. Is he being an awful trial?'

'No more than usual,' he lied. 'Were there any callers today? Somehow our social life seems to be as abominably dull as the weather this summer. Now why should that be, do you suppose?'

'I've really no idea, but it does seem so!' Harriet agreed, determined to match his light manner. 'But no, no one did call, unless you count old Lady Brent.'

'I don't!'

'I did have a note, though, from Miss Marwood,' she said tentatively.

He guessed her sister was feeling guilty about that lady's visit, so he prompted her. 'Well, and what does she have to say? I thought we might have seen something more of the Marwoods lately, since we're to be connected by marriage,' he added casually, but did not want to appear to press Harriet into inviting them in the circumstances, so he did not pursue that line.

'It seems we may have lost our opportunity, now.' Harriet could not keep the note of relief from her voice. 'They are travelling into Kent in a few days' time. Sir Ralph, it seems, is anxious to return home and his sister is posting down to Portsmouth . . . with Mrs Grimsby.'

'Yes, I kn — ' Roland choked hastily, then muttered: 'Too much spice in this meat sauce!' He had nearly revealed his visit to Mrs Grimsby: he would have to be careful, but he was not used to having secrets from Harriet. 'Yes, I am not surprised — I think Sir Ralph finds his town visits a sore trial.'

'Well, he has no call to stay here, now, has he? With both daughters promised, I mean,' she added in brittle tones.

'Harriet, love, there is no confirmation for that except the word of that knuckle-head brother of ours.'

'It's very sweet of you, but I have faced up to it now, you know. It was as plain as a pikestaff that that was the way of things, to anyone of the meanest intelligence. Besides, we haven't seen much of — ' she hesitated at the name, then said, 'The Grimsbys, of late, have we?'

'Ned is in Northamptonshire, remember, and I suppose his mother is preparing to travel down to Plymouth, or wherever.'

Harriet gave a wry and somewhat bitter laugh.

'You are a brave trier, I'll say that for you! All that means is that she is living in the Marwoods' pockets prior to their marriage connexion.'

It was no use, he could not stand aside and see his sister and his dear friend drift into such a disastrous situation. For, whatever Mrs Grimsby had said about not meddling in Ned's affairs, it was pretty clear to him that she was now set upon his marrying

Miss Marwood. It was understandable she should encourage the match when Ned's hopes were dashed by Harriet, but to continue to do so when she now knew it was not so . . . Roland was only just realizing the vindictiveness of her decision. No, it should not be, if he could prevent it!

'I'll have a wager with you that Miss Marwood does not marry Ned!' He would ride to Chelbeck on some pretext or other and see Ned whilst he was in Northamptonshire. He could leave town now with a little easier conscience, too, since Sophia Marwood was to be taken out of Piers' reach (he was glad Miss Marwood had contrived that) and Piers was, he assumed, safely occupied until the Charger's launching, in any event.

'I would not take your money, it would be robbery!' Harriet told him bluntly.

'Very well — but we shall see! Harriet,' he said a moment later, 'I was wondering if I should ride into

Northamptonshire for a day or two — Beechers seems to be in a greater lather than usual over the farms — but I don't care to leave you here on your own . . . '

To his great surprise, she laughed.

'You've no idea how opportune that is for you! You didn't know did you? No, how could you — I had the letter only today.'

'What are you talking about?'

'Augusta — she is coming up to town . . . '

'With the *infantry* in tow?' he asked fearfully.

'Yes, with little Jane and Sarah,' she confirmed in severe accents, 'and of course they must stay here.'

'Indeed, they must!' agreed Roland. 'As long as I am fixed at Chelbeck at the time that is — at least a hundred miles away from those two sticky-fingered horrors of hers!'

'That is no way to speak of your dear little nieces! But I must own, I am relieved you suggested going home for a space — I did not know how to broach the news to you!'

For the next few days, Roland felt happier — or as happy as anyone could who had to face a ride of a hundred miles through intermittent rain and over muddy roads: he was reasonably confident that even Piers could not do anything precipitate with regard to his marriage just at the moment, and at least he was acting on Harriet's behalf at last . . .

He bent his head, spurred his horse on, and hoped Ned would still be in Northamptonshire when he finally arrived there.

★   ★   ★

About the time Lord Bittadon dismounted at his ancestral home, Chelbeck Park, for a change of dry clothing before immediately pressing on the further few miles to Ned's estate, Emily was reading the announcement in the *Morning Chronicle* of his brother's forthcoming marriage.

Before Aunt Ashton had departed for Portsmouth, and the Marwoods returned to Hollsted, agreement had been reached that Sophia's betrothal should be announced publicly. Emily's protests that there was no haste, met, as she expected, with little sympathy — indeed, why should they? The parties involved were content with the situation and that was all that counted.

Sophia had been somewhat cast down by subsequent events after her undeniably unsatisfactory proposal from Mr Aubery. He had not been seen nor heard of since, and although this was put down to the fact that he was understandably busy with the stage-coach affairs, she had regarded their return into Kent as a conspiracy to keep them apart. However, although Emily had not discouraged the move to quit town early, circumstances had dictated it rather more than she had. When Aunt Ashton announced her intention of going to Portsmouth to meet her son George, the two girls were thus deprived of their chaperon: although this was a drastic step the match-making lady would not have contemplated it had she not been convinced both her charges were settled. From her long coses with Mrs Grimsby she had surmised what her son's intentions were towards Emily, and she was satisfied from the occasional remark of her niece that his suit would be successful. So Mrs Ashton set off to Portsmouth with a light heart and the comfortable sensation of a task well done.

Emily had just set aside the newspaper, with a rather less light-hearted feeling, when Sophia burst into the room with a return of her old boisterousness.

'Look, Emmy, isn't this fine?' She unrolled a handbill announcing, in varying dimensions of print, that the Chelbeck Charger would set out from the Spread Eagle in Gracechurch Street at 7 am on Mondays and Thursdays for

Dover, taking up passengers for Rochester, Sittingbourne and Ashford only: and returning on Tuesdays and Fridays.

Emily could not but be interested in this as, she had to admit, it was not every day one was involved in the birth of a stage-coach.

'It is not following the Dover Road all the way, then?' she commented, noting that Ashford and not Canterbury was on its route.

'No, Mr Aubery has explained it to papa in a letter. He is coming across the Downs from Sittingbourne, calling at our Hollsted Inn, and then down to the Ashford Road. It is something to do with having less stops than the ordinary coaches,' she added vaguely, as she frowned at the sheet.

'In the winter months I foresee he will have one stop only — on the top of the Downs in a snow-drift!' Emily said drily.

But her sister swept aside this distant drawback, and her plump face lit up suddenly. 'I'm to travel on the first run of the Charger on Monday, Emmy! Mr Aubery has sent a special ticket just for me, and he's to pick me up at the Hollsted Inn! You can come and watch, if you like,' she said as an afterthought.

'But where is he taking you?' Emily asked, stricken with the gravest fears — could this be Mr Aubery's elopement plan already?

'Only to the first inn along the Ashford road, where he changes horses, then I have to come back in a chaise with one of the other ladies on the coach,' she concluded grumpily.

'But has papa agreed to your going?' Emily was not greatly assured by the unknown lady's presence.

'Well, of course he has! It's a tremendous honour, don't you see? The very first run of the Chelbeck Charger ... ' she said in dreamy accents.

'I think someone ought to accompany you — if not I, Jenny, perhaps.' Although as she said this, Emily realized it was hopeless.

'There will be at least *half-a-dozen* people with me in the coach,' Sophia explained pityingly, 'and they will all have very special invitations.'

Emily did not give up entirely until she had seen her father, but then she accepted defeat.

'I think it most considerate of Mr Aubery to have arranged all this for Sophia,' Sir Ralph said. 'After all, he will have an empty seat for most of the first journey, won't he, just so that she may travel a few miles with him.'

Such a sacrifice merely increased Emily's suspicions but she had no one to turn to for advice. Then she remembered Lord Bittadon! *He* would be travelling in the coach, of course, on this first trip — he would keep an eye on his brother . . .

Piers, though, had hastened the birth of the Chelbeck Charger once he heard Roly was to be out of town. It presented him with a good excuse for leaving him off the first way-bill: he did not want his lordship casting a baleful eye over everything and ruining what promised to be a rewarding occasion.

The morning his betrothal appeared in the newspapers — although he was unaware of the momentous announcement himself — Piers was at Dartford at the Bull Inn, where he had taken to buying the drivers their ale, or rum and milk, so that he might exchange coaching tales with them. It gave him the sense of being one of their fraternity already, to listen to their stories of the craft of coaching — and much play was made of the mysteries of 'springing a team', 'chopping', 'towelling' and such like skills. Those Nestors of the road were quite willing to be exploited in this way, for they knew well who the gentleman was and, in the way of the experienced professional, were looking forward to witnessing the inevitable downfall of the foolish amateur.

In one of the brief intervals when there were no coaches changing horses at the Bull Inn, Piers took the opportunity of calling upon another place, where he was not quite so well-known in the town. He turned into an alley-way, looked up at the sign swinging outside, and mounted some dark stairs. A scrawny boy, clutching a bundle of papers with remarkably inky hands, suddenly debouched on to the small landing almost sending Piers back the way he had come.

'Is your master in, boy?' Piers asked, recovering his balance.

'Ay, sir! In there!' The printer's devil cheerfully jerked his head at one of the two doors, and disappeared down the stairs.

A few minutes later his master was looking at Piers dubiously over the top of his spectacles.

'I take it this is some sort of a hoax, sir? What I mean to say, is that I should not like responsibility for this (he tapped the paper) in any way.' He did not want to offend the fine gentleman but he had to be careful: his name would appear on the handbill, and he did not like the smell of the business afoot.

'Yes, to be sure it is!' Piers assured him irascibly. 'It's to do with a wager I'm having with my town friends.' The printer's face still looked doubtful. 'Look, I'll pay you double your usual rates — cash,' he added with reluctance, knowing how little of *that* he had left. 'All I want of you, is that announcement printed on two handbills.'

'Two sir? Why 'tis hardly worth settin' up the type.'

'Well, make it worthwhile, then! Besides, it proves I'm not going to blazon it all over the town, doesn't it?'

The printer nodded.

'Yes, sir . . . I suppose it does that.'

So the deal was concluded, and Piers went down the dingy stairs confident that he had made the first move towards turning his disastrous proposal of marriage to some immediate benefit.

11

When Mrs Knowle saw in her daily newspaper that her spendthrift rab-shackle nephew, Piers, was to marry the corky young daughter of Sir Ralph, her first reaction was disbelief. Then she called to mind the aunt in charge of the girls — as weak as water gruel, that was obvious! Then there was Sir Ralph; what was he thinking of to let a gel of his throw herself away on a wastrel like that? Well, he had clearly had the wool pulled over his eyes by that young whipper-snapper. She imagined he was indulging the fancies of his moon-struck daughter, too: she recalled how Sophia had gazed at Piers when first she had seen the two girls at Bittadon House.

What freak had come into Bittadon's noddle to allow this marriage of his coxcomb half-brother? (For she never thought of that boy as an Aubery) Mrs Knowle gave a sympathetic snort of laughter. No, she could scarcely blame Bittadon for wanting to get that rapscallion off his back, and besides — she did some rapid calculations — the boy was of age now, and out of his brother's command. Something had to be done, though, that was certain, and in a brace o'snaps, if she knew anything about her resty nephew. She glanced at the print again to make sure there was no date given for the wedding.

Well, she thought, it was time she had a spell of ruralizing — the weather in Kent could scarcely be worse than it was in London, and at least she could play whist with Sir Ralph once she had set him straight about his future son-in-law.

When the letter announcing Mrs Knowle's impending visit arrived at Hollsted Manor, Sir Ralph was delighted, Emily alarmed — and Sophia indifferent, largely because it was Monday and already she had donned her best carriage dress of blue shot sarcenet, and had changed her bonnet three times: on each occasion appealing to Emily for her opinion as to whether it was more suitable for the very first journey of a stage-coach than its predecessor.

However, Mrs Knowle was due to descend upon them on the coming Thursday — a day when Emily and Sophia had an invitation to ride over to the other side of the village and spend the day with the squire's two daughters, long-standing friends of the Marwoods. Emily felt it was incumbent upon her to stay and welcome Mrs Knowle, but Sophia had no such compulsion and announced she would go to the squire's as planned.

At last, that Monday morning, Sophia's patience was rewarded and the two sisters rode to the Hollsted Inn. They joined the small group of villagers who had gathered to see the arrival of the splendid new coach. Any stage-coach was a rarity in those parts and already numerous tales of the wonders of the Chelbeck Charger were abroad.

'Solid gold 'andles on the doors, I 'ear tell!' said one.

'Naw, nivver, not on a stage! But, mark you, I do know as 'ow it's got blinds of silk velvet and lace!' pronounced another.

Sophia exchanged a nervous smile with her sister as they listened to these extravagant claims. They had left their mounts in the inn stables and were waiting — with the villagers at a respectable distance — in the forecourt of the old black-and-white timbered hostelry.

'I do so hope he isn't late,' Sophia said anxiously. 'What time is it, do you have your watch?'

'No, but don't fret, I expect there's bound to be delays on the first run — everyone will want to congratulate Mr Aubery.' And ply him with rum.

thought Emily, knowing what a reputation for insobriety coachmen had.

The villagers, who used no clock but the sun, were content to wait indefinitely for such a momentous event . . .

'I can 'ear the 'orn!' cried one sharp-eared member of the crowd.

Emily quickly checked with Sophia the time she anticipated she would be home again.

'Never mind that, Emmy, I can see the coach!'

There was a long downward hill to the inn, and there could be no doubt, Emily had to admit, that Mr Aubery was a nonpareil of drivers, whatever his faults might be. The Chelbeck Charger stopped to the inch when it had seemed inevitable the team of four powerful horses must sweep past them.

Emily felt the excitement of the occasion more than she had expected, and found herself greeting Mr Aubery with unreserved cordiality.

Piers was polite in return although he

could never feel cordial again to Miss Marwood.

'Now, ma'am,' he said to Sophia, 'your ticket, if you please.' He took it, then with a flourish raised her hand to his lips . . . 'Well now, we've no time to linger! Up you get!' He opened the door for her.

On witnessing these special courtesies from the driver, a murmur of appreciation and astonishment ran through the crowd — who had no notion, of course, that the pair were a betrothed couple.

Emily quickly scanned the faces in the dim interior as the door of the coach was opened, but she could not see Lord Bittadon's among them!

She turned to Mr Aubery who was already clambering back onto the box. 'I had thought your brother would be with you, sir?'

'No, Bittadon is out of town, ma'am,' he told her cheerfully, taking up the reins. Then: 'Let 'em go!' he cried, and the ostler, who had had the privilege of standing by the leaders' heads, jumped out of the way just in time.

As the coach drew away the over-awed spectators raised a ragged cheer, but until that point they had conversed in whispers in the presence of such a gleaming, splendid vehicle.

Emily, her apprehensions fully returned now over the wisdom of letting Sophia go with Mr Aubery, bade the ostler fetch her horse, and she went home knowing she would not be easy until the next two hours were passed, and Sophia was safely back again.

★ ★ ★

Lord Bittadon had met with a setback when he had arrived, very weary ofter his long wet ride from London, at Ned's country house. The housekeeper there met him with the news that her master had left only that morning, and although he was making his way back to town she felt sure he was calling upon an old friend in Oxford on the way.

So, there seemed nothing for it but for Roland to spend at least a day or two at Chelbeck, soothing Beechers and reassuring him that responsibility for the bad hay harvest would not be laid at his door: although he felt that *he* was the one who stood in need of commiseration, all things considered. Another depressing chore looming ahead was his inspection of the parkland which, it seemed almost inevitable now, would be given over to mineral mining in the near future.

He toyed with the idea of sending a letter to Ned at Clarges Street but decided against it — for what could he say which would not look deuced odd on paper? No, if he returned to town himself soon he must be hard on the heels of Ned . . .

★　★　★

Sophia returned home as good as her word from her exciting expedition aboard the Chelbeck Charger, making

Emily feel somewhat guilty for entertaining such dark suspicions. Indeed, the brief reunion with her betrothed seemed to have rendered Sophia much happier than at any time since Mr Aubery's proposal, and Emily realized how mean-spirited she had been to try to deny her sister this innocent pleasure. Amidst rapturous descriptions of her afternoon out she did not quite forget Mrs Knowle's impending arrival, which also pleased Emily.

'Mrs Knowle does come Thursday, does she not?' Sophia confirmed with her sister. 'I did not have much time to talk with Mr Aubery, of course — only while they poled up new horses, and that was done with such amazing speed, you would not believe! — but he was interested to hear his aunt was to stay with us.'

Sir Ralph, who had been much cheered by the prospect of having Mrs Knowle to talk to in place of his colourless sister, Mary, could not hear enough about the Charger's progress.

To Emily's surprise he had accepted the fact that Mr Aubery was actually driving the coach himself, with amazing complacency. She wondered hopelessly what it would need to set him against that gentleman — he seemed almost as besotted as his daughter.

'Have you sent a message to Kate and Julia telling them I shall be visiting them on Thursday?' Sophia asked Emily the following day, again displaying an interest in everyday affairs which was something quite new in her.

'Yes, I did so this morning — I explained it was unavoidable that I should stay here to greet our unexpected visitor. I am sure they will understand.'

When Thursday came, Emily, who was in sole charge of the Manor staff now, was fully occupied ensuring that Mrs Knowle's room should be ready, her bed aired, fires laid, her maid catered for, as well as her coachman and groom, and, at Sir Ralph's insistence, enough food prepared for a marching army.

The sisters had their own rooms at the Manor so that Emily saw Sophia only briefly at breakfast that morning, and then again, a short time later, when Sophia put her head round the door to the linen room, where Emily was consulting with their housekeeper, Mrs Young.

'I'm going now, Emmy! I hope you enjoy your dinner with the old trout!' she said jauntily, then disappeared, leaving her sister to meet the disapproving stare of Mrs Young at such disrespectful language.

Mrs Knowle arrived exactly when she said she would, which pleased Sir Ralph who set great store by punctuality and order; and immediately, it seemed, the lofty dark-panelled rooms and passages were alive with activity and noise. If a dozen guests had arrived it would scarcely have caused more disturbance, thought Emily, although it was not unpleasant to have the Manor enlivened in this way: there was no denying it could be monstrously sepulchral at times.

When her lusty voice had ceased echoing about the house, Mrs Knowle was guided to the dining-hall, where her equally lusty appetite made short work of every dish set before her. Sir Ralph again was delighted, for he was a spare eater himself and enjoyed seeing someone else relish their victuals.

The talk centred upon her journey from town, her frank impressions of Hollsted Manor, and who could be called upon in the neighbourhood to make up a whist party — no mention was made of Sophia's forthcoming entry into the Aubery family. Indeed, when apologies were made for Sophia's temporary absence from home, Mrs Knowle, instead of expressing regret at the news, said: 'Capital! Capital!' in a mystifying way, and attacked the pigeon pie with renewed vigour.

Emily was given to understand that their visitor wished to talk privately with Sir Ralph as soon as she might

after dinner, so she excused herself
— quite happily as there was still plenty
needing her attention — and left the
two of them on their own.

It was six o'clock when Twell told
Emily that her father wanted her
in the Pilgrims' Hall — a splendid
and ancient room specially opened up
in Mrs Knowle's honour, as it had
been over the centuries for the
travellers on the Pilgrims' Way to
Canterbury.

Mrs Knowle was well able to
withstand both the magnificence and
the scale of the huge leaded windows
and elaborately embossed plaster ceil-
ing, by wearing — unwittingly, as she
had never seen the vehicle — the
colours of the Chelbeck Charger:
purple crepe gown with gold cap and
gloves and scarlet satin half boots. Sir
Ralph, if more soberly clad, was no less
formal in white silk stockings and
old-fashioned breeches with a claret
cassimere tail-coat.

'Emily, my dear, do sit down,' Sir

Ralph said in subdued tones, 'I have some distressing news to impart.'

She listened whilst he related a few things of the damning things Mrs Knowle had told him about her nephew, Mr Aubery — although omitting the fact that he was not an Aubery at all.

'I do not believe Miss Marwood is entirely set back on her heels by all this, are you, m'dear?' barked Mrs Knowle startlingly into the silence which followed.

But Emily did not relish being right in this instance, and said: 'My views in the affair are irrelevant, I fear, but what of Sophia?'

'She must be told at once,' Sir Ralph replied, 'and I shall write to Mr Aubery crying off for her. It is the greatest misfortune the announcement has already been made to the world, but that can be retracted.'

'It wasn't entirely a misfortune, Sir Ralph, for if I had not seen the betrothal in the newspaper I should not be here now setting you straight about that young trimmer.'

'True, ma'am, very true, and I'm sure I shall stand in your debt for ever. I do not know how I could have been so blind! I blame myself ... that poor girl!' Then he raised his head suddenly and fixed his myopic, bushy-browed stare on Emily. 'Is Sophia returned yet? I must see her.'

'No papa, but she should be back at any time.'

Mrs Knowle retired to her room for a while to leave Sir Ralph to face his youngest daughter.

Emily waited with her father for Sophia's return, but not without considerable apprehension as to the consequences when Sophia should know the truth of her betrothed. However, her apprehension was directed in another channel when, by eight o'clock, she was still not home. Little wretch, thought Emily, I expect she is avoiding the 'old trout's' company as long as possible.

'Send one of the grooms to escort her home,' Sir Ralph instructed at last, 'I'll not have her abroad on her own at this time of night.'

But the groom returned with the disquieting news that not only had Sophia not spent that day with Kate and Julia but she had scarcely been expected there after the receipt of her note earlier in the day. The groom had the note with him to prove the story, and Sophia, it seemed, had excused herself on the grounds of Mrs Knowle's visit.

Brice, the lady's maid, was summoned before the triumvirate of Sir Ralph, Mrs Knowle and Emily, and questioned. She told them Sophia had left quite openly with a portmanteau of clothing.

'She explained, sir, that she wanted to show some of her newly-acquired London dresses to the Miss Merridews.'

After the maid was dismissed Emily cried suddenly: 'It's Thursday! The

Chelbeck Charger runs through Hollsted today, doesn't it?'

'Well, there you are!' put in Mrs Knowle decisively, 'we need look no further — that young snirp of a nephew of mine has carried her off, you may depend upon it!'

Emily was immensely grateful for Mrs Knowle's presence: that was her conclusion also, but she would never have convinced her father of it on her own.

'Oh, no!' he said in appalled accents, 'I cannot believe that of the fellow . . . Great heavens, no!'

But Mrs Knowle swept aside this protest and took matters firmly in hand: a man was sent at once to the Hollsted Inn to see if Sophia's horse was stabled there. He returned with the mount and confirmation that the young owner had departed on the state-coach, bound for Dover. No stir had been caused by this at the inn, as the young lady had done exactly the same thing only a few days earlier with her sister in attendance.

'We must send after her before it is too late! They could be wed at any time if Mr Aubery has a special licence!' Sir Ralph exclaimed with great foreboding.

'I cannot argue with you,' Mrs Knowle remarked, 'but I do not see that fribble of a boy planning anything so far ahead. This will be a spur of the moment rig, mark my words! Nonetheless, send off your men after the runaways, if you wish, but where will you have them look?' she asked bluntly. 'All over Kent and London?'

'The coach makes a return journey tomorrow to London,' Emily reminded them.

Mrs Knowle snorted. 'Then you may rest assured the Honourable Piers will not be on the driving box! He will have someone to take over the driving for him.'

'What do you suggest we do, then, ma'am?' Sir Ralph appealed to her, quite out of his depth.

'Send Emily to town to see Bittadon,

post-haste!' came the immediate response. 'He's the only one who might
know how to deal with that boy and his
freaks. Lord knows, he's had experience
and plenty over the years! You may
take my carriage and driver, my dear.'
(She had seen Sir Ralph's antiquated
vehicles and coachman.) 'You'll be
there in the shake of a dice, and
Bittadon ought to know about this
latest antic as soon as possible, in any
event.'

Emily was fully in accord with this
proposition, and relieved she could act
in some way, but her father, unused to
such decisive methods, raised his voice
to object: 'But Emily cannot travel
alone all that way!'

'Fiddlesticks, I'm sure she won't
mind, will you, m'dear? But take your
maid by all means if you must,'
conceded Mrs Knowle to her host's
old-fashioned notions. 'As long as you
are running it by first light tomorrow,
that's all that counts. We have lost
enough time already.'

So it was arranged, and Emily found herself, after scarcely a wink of sleep, on the Dover Road in the grey dawn light: it was only then that she remembered Mr Aubery telling her that his brother was out of town . . .

* * *

But Roland had returned to Bittadon House late the night before, and had risen early to present himself at Ned's door after breakfast: he was determined to find him this time.

However, he had scarcely started upon his own solitary breakfast (Augusta and the brats were gone, he had discovered with relief, and Harriet had not risen yet) when Peck came in, in unusual haste.

'Mr Grimsby, my lord.'

Ned was in the room before the words were out of the butler's mouth.

'Thank God you're here, Bittadon! I must talk to you, alone.'

Roland dismissed the footman, but

could not take his eyes off his visitor: because for anyone who was acquainted with the imperturbable ex-campaigner of Wellington's army, Ned's bearing this morning was quite extraordinary. His eyes were dark-ringed, and he kept rubbing them as if he could not believe he was awake; he was unshaven and his riding boots were coated with mud.

'My dear fellow you look as though you haven't slept in a bed since lord knows when!'

'Nor have I — last night, in any event! I was riding all night from Oxford — only arrived at Clarges Street this morning at six, and then I had to come straight here.'

'Well, sit down and take some breakfast at least — '

Ned slumped into the chair next to Roland, and said in a desperate manner: 'No time for food — you must see this! Something has to be done!' He fished in a back pocket of his tail-coat and brought out two pieces of paper. 'These arrived for me when I was away — yesterday I believe — God knows what it all means: and why it was sent to *me*, I can't imagine! Perhaps you can explain! You'd best read the letter first.'

'But how should I know what it is all about, if it is directed to you?' Roland asked, taking the letter with some apprehension.

'Because it is from your brother, Piers,' Ned said, with a note of utter disgust in his voice.

12

Roland, having heard Piers was involved, could understand why Ned had come to him, but it scarcely explained his friend's trepidation over the matter — whatever it was.

He read the letter aloud quickly, being, accustomed to his brother's convoluted hand.

' 'Dear Ned, I approach you with a certain diffidence, but am persuaded you will be only too anxious to assist when you perceive it is in your best future interests.' ' Roland glanced at Ned in response to the hint of menace contained in this opening sentence, but his companion just shrugged his shoulders helplessly.

' 'My request concerns Miss Sophia Marwood (now, perhaps, you begin to understand?) who is at present in my custody.' ' Here Roland's jaw hardened and his expression became very grim. ' ' . . . It is her belief that I am waiting to obtain a special licence so that we may be wed with greater expedition than her parent will allow, but this is not my intention. The betrothal was an act of folly, and I have no wish to crown it with an even greater one by marrying her.' '

Ned, still greatly upset, cried: 'I had no idea they were betrothed even!'

Roland continued his reading, not knowing what to expect next from this alarming document. ' 'However — and this is where I count upon you to use your good offices with my brother — the young lady will be returned to the bosom of her family only when I am in receipt of the sum of four thousand pounds from him. (He will know the significance of this amount).'

'The devil I do!' ground out Roland between his teeth. 'He has the nerves to demand his marriage settlement for a kidnap!'

Then he resumed with the letter.

' 'You may reassure him that he need entertain no fears that any further requests . . . ' *Requests!* ' . . . will be received from me after this exchange, on any account whatsoever, for it is my intention to quit these shores the instant I receive the monies with which to set forth on my travels.

' 'The bulk of the money may be in the form of a banker's order, drawable upon a Paris bank for ease of payment — and the added assurance for Roland that I do intend to leave the country (and never return)' He's mad, Ned, raving mad!'

'Read on,' Ned advised with both weariness and pity in his voice.

' 'I have no desire to distress Miss Sophia Marwood unduly and so wish to complete this transaction with the utmost speed. If he will take a packet containing the *full* amount of the money to the Spread Eagle in Gracechurch Street by noon on Friday . . . ' Today!' cried Roland. ' ' . . . the driver of the Dover Mail, due to depart a half

266

hour later, has instructions to receive it.' Well, I have not lost my wits too! I shan't do it, of course. I must inform the Runners — it should not present any insuperable difficulty to trace — '

'You do not know the whole, yet,' Ned cut in. 'See the closing paragraphs.'

After a brief look of alarm at his friend, Roland continued: ' 'I am sure he will not hesitate to act to save a lady's reputation, and ensure the departure of his 'brother' from his ken — but in case he should do so I enclose a handbill for his perusal. An entertaining notion, is it not, and should cause not a little stir about the streets of London when it is circulated — on Saturday morning!'

'Is that it in your hand?' Roland asked Ned. 'Let me have it.'

It was handed over reluctantly.

Odd words on the large type met Roland's eyes, then he read the whole. ' 'Of interest to those GENTLEMEN in SEARCH of a WIFE — a most

HIGH-BRED YOUNG LADY will be OFFERED to the HIGHEST BIDDER by a HUSBAND desirous of a CHANGE. The sale to take place close by THE AUCTION MART, in St. Bartholomew's Lane . . . ' ' He stopped at this point and muttered, 'I don't believe it.'

'No, nor did I . . . I'm sorry. I thought he had run mad.'

'I'm the one to be sorry, it's *my* fiend of a brother, isn't it?' Roland said savagely. 'And I can't tell you how sorry I am, too, that you have been dragged into this unsavoury business at all.'

'But do you know why he should write to me? What does he mean by 'my best future interests'?' Ned entreated him.

'Well . . . I may do,' Roland said hesitantly, able at last to refer to the matter he had been anxious to discuss with his friend for so long — but under what circumstances now! 'I believe Piers is under the impression that it is your intention to marry into the

Marwood family yourself, and that therefore you would be most anxious to preserve the name from any breath of scandal.'

Ned's tired brown eyes, watched closely by his friend, betrayed no emotion. 'I presume he must refer to Miss Marwood,' he said slowly, 'but to the best of my knowledge I have neither said nor done anything which could have made him so confident. By God, I hope not, in any event!' he cried, in sudden agitation. 'I should not wish the lady herself to be under any misapprehension.'

Roland did not know, of course, how Piers had received this impression, but he did know Ned's own mother seemed to expect the match.

'I should not fret: Piers needed an intermediary in this dirty business of his, and doubtless he was anxious to fix upon as many susceptibilities as possible,' he said reassuringly.

'But *you* were aware of what he meant in his letter about my 'interests', were you not?' countered Ned at once.

Roland could hardly tell him he had been behind his back to his mother, so he said as casually as possible: 'A guess on my part, that is all — you did not seem wholly indifferent to Miss Marwood.'

Ned looked very unhappy. 'I have behaved foolishly by demonstrating such partiality, I admit it, but then I did not know . . . ' His voice tailed off.

'Did not know what?'

'Oh, never mind! What about your brother? We're wasting precious time!'

Roland could see Ned was almost at the end of his tether. 'That dreadful business can wait just a few more minutes. Tell me, what were you about to say?'

Ned looked about the room before he spoke, as if to ascertain that they were quite alone. 'I did not know I could never marry anyone but your sister. I deluded myself for a while, then I realized . . . ' He shrugged.

'Ask her again.'

Ned stared as if he did not understand what was being said.

' . . . And don't take no for an answer this time!' Roland grinned. 'I can't do with a lovesick female under my feet forever.'

'You are sure about this?' Ned asked slowly.

'As sure as one ever can be of the female of the species! Now you, my dear Ned, are going to have some breakfast, and then I shall put you into Judd's care. Rest an hour or two in my room until I return — unless, of course, you wish to see Harriet before then.'

'I can't see her looking like this!'

'I don't think she'll care a twopenny dam, quite frankly!' He pushed his chair back and gathered up the letter and the handbill. 'Now I have work to do, if you'll excuse me.'

'May I ask how you intend to act?'

'I haven't a vast amount of choice, have I? I shall send him his money and consider it a small price to pay to be rid of him.'

'But can you possibly trust him to keep his word? As long as he has the girl — '

'I don't think he will linger when he has the money. He is, if my suspicions are correct, up to his ears in debt, and I am well aware he is bequeathing those to my care as well,' said Roland bitterly. 'The girl has nothing to fear from him, I would hazard, she is merely a means to an end . . . Everyone is to Piers.'

* * *

After one of their horses had cast a shoe just east of Rochester, Emily began to wonder if she should turn back to Hollsted. After all, if Lord Bittadon wasn't there when she arrived it would be a fruitless journey; but then she remembered Harriet who would, at least, know where to find her twin — if not her young brother.

It was one o'clock when the harassed coachman finally pulled up outside Bittadon House, and he thanked his stars it was not his mistress, Mrs Knowle, he had carried on this journey: he would have had the rough side to her tongue for his pains, and that was an experience to be avoided at all costs . . .

Emily told him she had no idea when she would be returning to Hollsted and that he must await orders. She then mounted the steps, assailed with anxieties as to whether Lord Bittadon would be there — what he could do to help matters if he was — and finally, the constant worry of the past twelve hours or more, what *had* happened to poor Sophia by this time?

Roland was in the hall when the visitor was admitted: he was putting off his riding gloves and had clearly just returned home himself.

'Miss Marwood!' he said, before Peck had time to utter. 'Are you alone?'

'Yes, I — '

'Good,' Roland cut in briskly. 'I think I know the purpose of your visit, but if you will step into the bookroom, we can talk.'

She could not imagine how he knew about Sophia but her relief was enormous: she had been afraid he would be as mystified as they were over the whole affair.

'It is about your sister and my brother you have come, I collect?' Roland said as soon as the door closed upon them. 'Yes, I thought so, and I must apologise most humbly, first of all, for the distress our family has brought upon yours.'

'But do you know where they are? Are they married?'

'No, but . . . ' He drew a hand across his forehead. 'This is hard to explain, I'm afraid, but your sister has been duped into going with Piers — she imagined they were eloping and they were not.'

'But what, then?' Emily cried in some alarm. 'What are you trying to tell me?'

'I'm sorry — I don't mean to agitate you — rather the contrary. It is difficult, I find, to explain my brother's actions to anyone who does not know him

— and this latest treachery is beyond *his* customary conduct. His prime objective in life is always to extract the last penny from any situation he finds himself in. In this instance, he has taken your sister into custody, as he puts it, until a sum of money is paid over to him, then she will be released.'

'Kidnapping! I don't believe it!'

'No, I cannot blame you,' Roland said sadly. 'I have never known him sink so low. He is, I have reason to believe, in desperate straits at the moment.'

'And what of Sophia — is she not in desperate straits, too?' she countered sharply.

'Your sister will be returned home tomorrow on the Dover Mail — I have his word upon that.'

'His word!' repeated Emily scathingly. 'And what worth has that, pray? The money has been paid then?' she added in calmer tones.

'Yes, I had no alternative if your sister's good name was to be preserved.' Miss Marwood should never know with what Piers had threatened her sister, though. 'As to the value of his word, I believe it is essential for him to leave the country as soon as possible. Indeed, he says he will be sailing on the Dover packet tomorrow — he has innumerable debts which can probably be evaded no longer.'

When Roland had delivered the packet that morning as instructed to the driver of the Dover Mail, he had been given a further letter from Piers in exchange. It was no less distasteful than the first one directed to Ned, and totally without remorse.

'Dear Roly, I knew I could count on you! And you may count on me, of course. The money should be in my hands by Friday evening and when it is, I shall leave all necessary instructions for Miss Sophia Marwood to be returned home by the Dover Mail on Saturday morning. There has been nothing in my treatment of her which need give you or her family a moment's disquiet. She has been lodged in a most reputable inn under the eye of the landlady — ostensibly awaiting the arrival of her nearest and dearest from the continent. You will not hear from me again. My best love to Harriet. I fancy she will be the only one to lament my going. Goodbye. Piers.

'P.S. I bequeath you the Chelbeck Charger: two splendid fellows have the care of it — their wages are due at the end of the week.'

No, it was not a letter which he would choose to show to Miss Marwood: she would have to take his word for it.

'He is leaving the country?' said Emily. 'You are sure of that? He is not taking Sophia with him?'

'I am as sure of it as I have ever been of anything my brother has done: and no, he will not be taking your sister with him.' (He would not want a female hindering his continental adventures, of that he was certain.)

As for the threat of the auction, Roland thought Piers was bluffing over that because he would have faced certain arrest himself had he appeared at the Auction Mart. However, he had had no wish to push his brother to the borders of desperation: he might just be vicious enough to drag everyone down with him in those circumstances . . .

'I feel I should have prevented this happening in some way,' Roland told his visitor, 'but I did not foresee the diabolical turn my brother's scheming would take.'

'No, how could you?' she said fairly, but she was still stunned by the villainy of Mr Aubery, even after Mrs Knowle's revelations — which had after all concerned his financial irresponsibilities only.

'Tell me, what was the marriage settlement your father had fixed upon Sophia, do you know?'

Emily explained the broad details, including the thirty thousand pounds due to her sister in seven years' time.

Seven years! No, there was no need to look any further than that for the root of Piers' actions: but Roland still did not know why his choice had not fallen upon the elder sister if financial gain was his only motive. Well, that he would never discover now, but everything else was explained if not excused.

'Forgive me! I have offered you no refreshment and you must be worn to the bone with anxiety, not to mention your long journey from Kent. You came in your father's carriage?'

'No, Mrs Knowle's. Indeed, I came here at her suggestion — papa, I am perfectly sure, would never have countenanced such a thing.'

'Aunt Knowle?'

'Yes, she is staying with us at Hollsted. She came post-haste after seeing Sophia's betrothal in her newspaper.'

'Newspaper? I am sorry to sound like a poll-parrot but I did not know the announcement had been made! That is regrettable.'

'I tried to dissuade the family from a premature public intimation but to no avail,' Emily said, feeling suddenly very tired.

'A further notice must be published at once, quashing the arrangement, and we must hope it will all be forgotten in a few weeks. And now I intend to put you in the venerable Treen's care — you have your own maid with you?'

'Oh yes! Papa insisted on that proviso in any event.'

Roland looked troubled. 'I must see your father as soon as possible. It is only fitting he should hear the truth from me.'

'You are travelling to Hollsted, my lord?'

'I must! I can in no way alleviate the distress already caused by my brother to your parent, but I must be on hand for Sophia's return tomorrow.'

'Or, in case she should *not* return . . . ?'

'I do think that an unlikely outcome — but I should prefer to be there come what may. Also, I wish to ride on to Dover later, to make sure my brother really did sail on the Dover packet when he stated. There can be no question of your returning into Kent today, but shall you be able to face another dawn start? If so, I will ride with your carriage.'

'Yes, of course. I am most anxious to be with papa again, as you may imagine.'

'You shall be.' Then on Treen's arrival, he added, 'Now, try and take a rest and I will see you at dinner, perhaps?'

Putting Miss Marwood into the maid's care reminded him that earlier he had put Ned into Judd's: really, he thought, Bittadon House is becoming a sanctuary for my brother's victims, but please God it is for the last time . . .

He went in search of Harriet and Ned.

They were together in the morning-room, and as soon as he saw Ned's face — quite transformed from the hagged expression he had worn earlier — he knew his friend had taken his advice.

Harriet also looked happier than he had seen her for months past, although when the felicitations were over she became suddenly sober.

'Tell me about Piers,' she appealed to her twin. 'Ned will only say he is in some scrape or other — but it's a serious one this time, isn't it?'

'Yes, love, I'm afraid it is.' Roland silently cursed his brother for inflicting this sorrow on Harriet, on what should have been her happiest day . . .

Ned did not stay for dinner, but promised to call at the house each day until Roland should return. It was agreed between brother and sister that Harriet's betrothal should be kept from Emily for the time being: neither knew how she would respond to it and did not care to add to her burdens at the moment.

Had they but known they could have been spared their anxieties, for Emily had finally accepted what she had suspected for some time — that she loved Lord Bittadon. She had first been aware of this when she spoke to him about Sophia and Piers; and her feelings were now quite powerful enough to place any idea of marrying Ned Grimsby out of her mind.

But she feared that, whatever the outcome of Mr Aubery's actions, she would see very little of his family in the future. Her father, quite understand-ably, would wish to cut the connexion with them . . .

Such were her gloomy thoughts as Roland escorted her back to Hollsted, although uppermost was her concern for Sophia, whose safe return was only half of her anxiety — what terrible consequences would follow upon the realization that Mr Aubery had spurned her, and used her merely as a pawn in his wicked stratagem to acquire money?

As they approached Hollsted, Roland drew level with the carriage window and sought to reassure her.

'Do not be anxious if your sister is not arrived home, for she scarcely could be: the Dover Mail will not have reached Sittingbourne yet.'

So, they were both confounded to see Sophia at the door to welcome them: she was, moreover, looking remarkably pleased with herself.

13

'Sophia, my love!' cried Emily as soon as she had clambered down from the carriage. 'Are you well? We have been so *worried!*'

'Of course I am,' her sister said dimissively, but at once cast a doubtful glance in Lord Bittadon's direction. 'Good morning, my lord,' she began formally, but then babbled: 'I hope you will explain to your brother that I am sorry for what I did in misleading him, but I could not bring myself to go through with it!'

Emily exchanged looks with her companion, but before he could reply to this baffling request Mrs Knowle joined the party.

'Miss Marwood! Bittadon! Do you come in!' she invited, just as if she were mistress of the manor. 'Well, it appears you have both been hurtling about the countryside to no avail! This little minx had everything in hand — once she came to her senses, that is. But there,' she said, ruffling Sophia's golden curls playfully but much to that young lady's annoyance, 'I always knew she was a sensible gel and must see through such a worthless fellow! ... I'm sorry, Bittadon, but there's no denyin' he is *that!*'

'No, ma'am, I'll not argue on that head now, I assure you,' he agreed grimly, wondering what colourful language the whole truth about Piers would bring forth from his aunt.

'But when did you arrive home, Sophia?' Emily asked, still utterly bewildered.

'Last night! Well, I could not tolerate another minute in that frightful inn waiting for Mr Aubery to return with his special licence. Besides, I had decided by then I did not want to marry him — ever — so it was all I could do, wasn't it?'

Once again glances passed between

Emily and Roland, but this time there was a dawning realization of what had happened.

'He had told the landlady I was his half-sister,' Sophia went on, 'so I left a note for him with her, explaining why I was leaving.'

Roland, the only one present who knew the full story, was speechless. That rogue, Piers, had the luck of the devil, and no mistake! He had clearly been utterly confident of the girl and hadn't given a thought to her escaping. But what if she had left sooner, say Thursday? No, that was the day she ran away, which would have been highly unlikely — so, perhaps he had not cared that she might escape later. If that were so it suggested he had had no real intention of implementing his bizarre auction threat. Certainly it would be charitable to assume that were the case: in any event only Ned and he knew anything of that — and only Harriet and Miss Marwood were aware of the ransom demand. He would prefer it to stay that way . . .

'. . . I can't tell you how pleased I am,' Emily was saying to her sister, 'and I daresay Lord Bittadon is too! I fancy he was not looking forward to searching the countryside for the pair of you, were you, my lord?' She threw caution to the winds and gave his lordship a hasty but unmistakable wink.

'Indeed I was not!' he confirmed wholeheartedly. 'Nor do I care greatly for horse-whipping brothers!' He bestowed upon Miss Marwood a look of the deepest gratitude: the ransom was to remain their secret evidently.

Emily's motives were not entirely unselfish: the less her father knew of the despicable episode the better — he might not then forbid a continuing friendship between the families . . .

Roland left that same night for Dover to make sure his brother really had fled to France, but before he went he snatched a few private moments with Emily. The events of the day had made them conspirators, and their brief discussion was given over mostly to ensuring they both held the same story about Piers — which was that Roland had known nothing of the 'elopement' except what Emily, and then Sophia, had told him. Ostensibly his trip to Dover was to verify Sophia's story of the inn where she had stayed, and also to bring his brother to heel if it were possible.

When these 'facts' were verified between them, Roland went on to explain Piers' parentage to Emily. He was then left with one final matter, about Harriet, which was a good deal more difficult to broach. However, there was little time at his disposal and he was anxious to know her response whatever it might be: he delayed no longer.

'There will be one quite proper marriage in our family, in any event. Harriet and Ned are to marry — probably quite soon.' He watched her face closely.

'Oh! I am pleased to hear that! They

always seemed so . . . *right* together. Some people do, don't they?'

Well, he thought, the news did not appear to have come as a severe blow, but after his experience with Harriet he had little faith in his discernment . . .

He rode off to Dover leaving a somewhat shattered Marwood family behind him. Sir Ralph suffered the greatest affliction, knowing it had been his misjudgment which had caused the whole unfortunate episode; but he had Mrs Knowle on hand to support his spirits.

Emily felt she had failed sadly in her efforts to protect her sister, and still shuddered at what might have befallen Sophia if Mr Aubery had been more determined in his efforts to marry her.

Sophia, though, except for the inevitable severe scolding from her father, felt she had fared rather well; because Emily, from whom she had expected a constant chiding, seemed amazingly understanding for once.

Mrs Knowle directed all her censure

to her young nephew, whom she really did want Bittadon to horsewhip when he found him.

It was almost a week later when his lordship returned, but everyone's anxieties were relieved when he gave the news that his brother had gone to France — except perhaps Mrs Knowle's, who had been looking forward to seeing just retribution fall upon the culprit at last.

Roland explained to the Marwoods and Mrs Knowle where his travels had taken him. ' . . . As soon as I discovered Piers had sailed on the Packet I decided I must ride to London with all despatch, in case he should have written to me. There was, in fact, a letter from him advising me of his intention to leave the country — '

'Oh! I had no notion he would take it so hard, truly I hadn't!' Sophia cried. 'Poor Mr Aubery, how dreadful!'

'Pray do not distress yourself, ma'am,' Roland bade her, but he feared that even a hint of the truth might be more hurtful for her to hear. 'My brother was grossly encumbered by debts and had little choice but to quit the country.'

Later, when Emily had been showing Mrs Knowle and her nephew the roses in the manor garden — which were late that summer — Mrs Knowle suddenly recalled it was time for Sir Ralph's physic.

Roland threw Emily a quizzical glance when the lady had departed. 'I trust my doughty relative is not usurping your duties?'

'Oh no! Papa would never take *any* dosing at my instigation, I assure you, but is as meek as a babe with Mrs Knowle!'

'That does astonish me!' he admitted, then turning to more serious matters, said: 'I hope you did not mind my equivocation earlier over the fate of my brother? It was borne in on me that I must explain my knowledge of Piers' plans, and by rearranging the order of events I was able to do so.'

'I am only too pleased it has proved possible to conceal the worst of the story,' Emily told him with genuine relief.

Roland echoed that sentiment in a heartfelt fashion, but he was thinking of the whole of the sordid tale, which was known only to Ned and himself.

He went on to tell her that the Chelbeck Charger, after a brief hour of glory, would run no more, but would finish its days as his family carriage. 'Quite the reversal of the customary fate of a coach, which often ends its days plying the stage routes,' he commented.

'The villagers will be disappointed to be deprived of such a colourful and exciting event — it made us feel quite important for a brief space,' Emily observed with a rueful smile.

'I am afraid you must regret the day you encountered Piers,' Roland said presently.

'Not entirely, for otherwise I should never have known Harriet . . . or you,' she told him, blushing slightly. 'But it was wholly a misfortune for you surely? The meeting appears to have precipitated your brother's ruin.'

'He was quite capable of doing that without any help! Besides, I must own, it is a great weight lifted from my mind to think that the Channel divides me forever from his escapades! . . . No, far from a misfortune, I have hopes I may be able to thank my brother for introducing me to my future wife.'

The change of tone caught Emily's attention and with her blue eyes fixed uncertainly upon him, he went on: 'In which case I should easily be able to forgive Piers for every undesirable acquaintance he has thrown in my way over the years, and even feel well rewarded for every scrape he has fallen into.' To remove any doubts she might have still, he added: 'Dear child though she is, I do not refer to Sophia, you know! I could never love her — or indeed anyone — as I have come to love you . . . '

His lordship, unaccustomed to making such an impassioned declaration, concluded with a nervous smile: 'Well, what do you say, will you redress the balance?'

Emily was glad of this final, nonsensical question, for it gave her time to take control of her reeling senses.

'I am not at all sure I care to be cast in the role of a weight! Indeed, I do not think I could marry for so shabby a reason!' Her audience looked so stricken at this point she dropped the bantering tone and, feeling suddenly solemn, went on: 'Yes . . . I will marry you . . . but because I love you — no other reason.'

After their first rapturous delight in discovering their mutual sentiments — for it appeared they had both fallen in love at precisely the same moment — Roland felt obliged to advert to Sir Ralph.

'One can scarcely expect him to be thrown into transports over another Aubery match,' he said doubtfully.

'Piers is only a half-brother,' Emily observed in a staunch fashion.

'Yes, but that is something exceedingly difficult to prove! For all your parent knows it is a convenient way of dissociating myself from him. We did share a mother, there's no denying that!'

'Well, I suggest we ask him without delay,' Emily said with resolution. 'Even if he disapproves the match he cannot prevent it, can he? We are both over age.'

'True, but I should not wish to be compelled to elope!'

Emily chuckled appreciatively. 'No, indeed! That would *not* serve in this case ... But what of Sophia?' she asked, suddenly reminded of her sister. 'I cannot leave her in Aunt Ashton's care, or papa's, after recent events, can I?'

'Frankly I think Sophia has shown more sense than her chaperons! And surely she must have learned her lesson now?'

'Perhaps you are right,' Emily agreed reluctantly. 'There is no doubt she displayed foresight in carrying money with her when she ran off — although I still wonder how she found herself a seat on the Mail-coach home at such short notice! I own I should not have known where to begin!'

'Exactly so! Your sister is a resourceful young lady, and it is my opinion she will go along famously now under your aunt's care.'

But Emily could not share this optimistic view and said so.

'If you are hinting that she should live with us after we marry, I confess I do not care for the notion,' he warned her gently.

'Oh no, nor do I! But I shall not be easy until I see some proof of her reformation.'

'Let us face one difficulty at a time!' Roland suggested, taking her hand. 'We will seek out your father before you discover any more problems.'

They found Sir Ralph alone.

'Ah, Emily, I was wondering where you had got to,' he began, a trifle querulously, in the manner of the abandoned house-bound. 'I wanted to have a word with you . . . No, my lord, I would be pleased if you would stay — my news concerns you, too, to some small degree.'

Convinced that their *own* news, now suppressed, *must* be more important than Sir Ralph's, the two young people exchanged frustrated smiles.

'Yes, papa, what is it?' Emily asked as patiently as she could.

'I had a letter from Mary in Portsmouth the other day, as you know, but what I omitted to tell you is that she is proposing to set up house with Mrs Grimsby — in Northamptonshire, I collect. She is well aware, of course, that her departure will throw us into a quandary here.'

Oh no, thought Emily, papa is surely not going to suggest I take sole charge of Sophia? Her spirits plunged.

'However,' continued Sir Ralph, with

a surprising, gruff laugh, 'she has in fact *rescued* me from a quandary! For I did not know how she and Mrs Knowle would go on together in the same house — being so very different in disposition, you know,' he added, explaining the obvious in his vague fashion.

'In the *same* house?' Emily repeated disbelievingly.

'Why, yes. For it is my intention to wed Mrs Knowle as soon as maybe. We deal together exceedingly well, and we are both agreed it will answer the best in every way. If, of course, you do not have any reservations in the matter, my dear?'

He turned apologetically to Roland. 'You will understand, my lord, I am sure, that in the circumstances my daughter might well be hesitant about any matrimonial connexion between our families.'

It was some time before their mirth could be explained to a highly puzzled Sir Ralph . . .

We do hope that you have enjoyed reading this large print book.

Did you know that all of our titles are available for purchase?

We publish a wide range of high quality large print books including:
Romances, Mysteries, Classics
General Fiction
Non Fiction and Westerns

Special interest titles available in large print are:
The Little Oxford Dictionary
Music Book, Song Book
Hymn Book, Service Book

Also available from us courtesy of Oxford University Press:
Young Readers' Dictionary
(large print edition)
Young Readers' Thesaurus
(large print edition)

For further information or a free brochure, please contact us at:
Ulverscroft Large Print Books Ltd.,
The Green, Bradgate Road, Anstey,
Leicester, LE7 7FU, England.
Tel: (00 44) **0116 236 4325**
Fax: (00 44) **0116 234 0205**

SUMMER IN HANOVER SQUARE

Charlotte Grey

The impoverished Margaret Lambart is suddenly flung into all the glitter of the Season in Regency London. Suspected by her godmother's nephew, the influential Marquis St. George, of being merely a common adventuress, she has, nevertheless, a brilliant success, and attracts the attentions of the young Duke of Oxford. However, when the Marquis discovers that Margaret is far from wanting a husband he finds he has to revise his estimate of her true worth.

CONFLICT OF HEARTS

Gillian Kaye

Somerset, at the end of World War I: Daniel Holley, unhappily married to an ailing wife and father of four grown-up children, is attracted to beautiful schoolteacher Harriet Bray, but he knows his love is hopeless. Daniel's only daughter, Amy, who dreams of becoming a milliner and is caught up in her love for young bank clerk John Tottle, looks on as the drama of Daniel and Harriet's fate and happiness gradually unfolds.

THE SOLDIER'S WOMAN

Freda M. Long

When Lieutenant Alain d'Albert was deserted by his girlfriend, a replacement was at hand in the shape of Christina Calvi, whose yearning for respectability through marriage did not quite coincide with her profession as a soldier's woman. Christina's obsessive love for Alain was not returned. The handsome hussar married an heiress and banished the soldier's woman from his life. But Christina was unswerving in the pursuit of her dream and Alain found his resistance weakening . . .

THE TENDER DECEPTION

Laura Rose

When Sophia Barton was taken from Curton Workhouse to be a scullery-maid at Perriman Court, her future looked bleak. Was it really an act of Providence that persuaded Lady Perriman to adopt her as her ward? Sophia was brought up together with the Perriman children, and before sailing with his regiment for India, George, the heir to the title, declared his love. But tragedy hit the family and Sophia found herself caught up in a web of mystery and intrigue.

CONVALESCENT HEART

Lynne Collins

They called Romily the Snow Queen, but once she had been all fire and passion, kindled into loving by a man's kiss and sure it would last a lifetime. She still believed it would, for her. It had lasted only a few months for the man who had stormed into her heart. After Greg, how could she trust any man again? So was it likely that surgeon Jake Conway could pierce the icy armour that the lovely ward sister had wrapped about her emotions?